Lily's Cowboys:
Second Chance Book 1

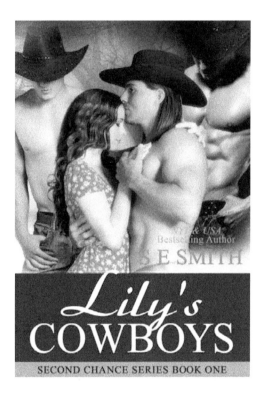

By S.E. Smith

Acknowledgments

I would like to thank my husband Steve for believing in me and being proud enough of me to give me the courage to follow my dream. I would also like to give a special thank- you to my sister and best friend Linda, who not only encouraged me to write but who also read the manuscript. Also to my other friends who believe in me: Julie, Jackie, Lisa, Sally, Elizabeth (Beth) and Narelle. The girls that keep me going!

—S.E. Smith

Montana Publishing

Paranormal Romance

LILY'S COWBOYS: SECOND CHANCE BOOK 1

Copyright © 2010 by S.E. Smith

First E-Book Published December 2010

Cover Design by Melody Simmons

Summary: Lily is reborn time after time to help families in need, only to die again once the families no longer need her, but the Cunnings brothers are determined to keep her for themselves.

ISBN: 978-1-942562-53-5 (paperback)

ISBN: 978-1-942562-16-0 (eBook)

Published in the United States by Montana Publishing.

{1. Paranormal Romance – Fiction. 2. Paranormal – Fiction. 3. Romance – Fiction.}

www.montanapublishinghouse.com

Synopsis

Sometimes life begins after you die. At least it has for Lily O'Donnell. Lily O'Donnell had always wanted to find a love as beautiful as her parents had. When her father suspiciously dies in an accident and her mother is brutally raped and murdered, Lily has to fight for her life. When she is trapped by the man who murdered both her parents and threatens to do to her what he did to her mother, Lily feels she has only one choice to avoid a fate worse than death.

Reborn to help others, Lily reappears time after time to help families in need, only to die again once the families no longer need her. Things change when Maggie Cunnings finally has enough of her three nephews' attitudes. Wanting to go home to sunny Florida and leave the frigid winters of Wyoming behind, Maggie prays for a little help in teaching the Cunnings brothers how to live and love again. The Cunnings men aren't the easiest to get along with. They've gone through six housekeepers in as many months. When Maggie hires Lily to be their new housekeeper sparks fly as the brothers and Lily learn that living and loving sometimes comes with no guarantees.

When a madman targets Lily, believing she has the knowledge to make him an immortal, the men have to come together as a family to help save the woman they love. Will they be able to save her and make her theirs, or will she once again be taken away?

Contents

Chapter 1
Sometimes life begins after you die.

Lily O'Donnell pulled her hat further down on her head, trying to protect her face as much as she could from the rain pouring down around her. She was drenched through to her skin and shivered as cold raindrops ran down under the collar of her jacket. She let out a tired sigh as she struggled.

Her long dress wasn't helping matters as it kept tangling around her legs, making each step on the three-mile journey from town to home even more difficult. Pulling the small basket of dry goods she had picked up at the general store closer to her, she was just thankful she was almost home. At almost eighteen, she had taken over most of the work around the farm she and her mother lived on outside of the small town of Oak Grove, Oklahoma. It was all they had left, and they were determined to keep it.

Her parents had moved out to Oklahoma twenty years before, wanting to make a new start away from the hectic life found in the city. It had been a difficult journey for her mother, but her father, Gerald O'Donnell, had wanted to find a place where he could farm and raise a family. Everything had been fine until two years ago when a man from town named James Butler had started coming around. Lily didn't like him. Butler had been trying to pressure her father into letting him marry her.

Lily's father had ordered the man away, but it was unnerving how often he still seemed to show up on or near their farm. When her father had died a year later in an accident while working with Butler, she had become suspicious and begged the sheriff to investigate. The sheriff could find no conclusive proof that Butler had anything to do with her father's fall off a barn roof they had been working on together at a nearby farm. Now with her father gone, Butler had begun pressuring Lily's mother, Maureen, to marry him. Lily's mother did what she could to discourage him, telling him over and over not to come around.

Lily sighed again as she thought of the last few months. It had been very hard for them. She and her mother knew living on a farm would be hard. What they had not expected to discover was that for two women living alone on a farm it was almost impossible, as the work and repairs were never ending.

To compound matters, in recent weeks James Butler had been more insistent about coming out, ignoring Lily and her mother's protests that neither of them needed nor wanted his help. Yesterday, he had hidden in their barn and grabbed Lily when she had gone out to gather eggs. He had smelled heavily of alcohol and sweat, making her cringe in fear.

She had fought him off, screaming when he grabbed her breast in a brutal grip, leaving dark, painful bruises behind. When she heard Lily's screams, her mother had rushed out of the house, clutching her husband's old shotgun to her chest. Butler had threatened them both, telling Maureen he was going to marry her whether she wanted to or not and that Lily was going to be his too. Maureen, small-boned and delicate, had stood there with the heavy gun pointed at his chest, fearlessly demanding he leave and not come back.

Lily had been hesitant to make the weekly journey to town, but they needed to get supplies and sell some of the items they had. So Lily had left early this morning to make the trip to town, hoping to be back before it began raining again. She took the items she and her mother had canned and fresh vegetables to Mr. Marshall at the local general store to help supplement their income once a week. They desperately needed the money, and Maureen had encouraged Lily to go, though it was against Lily's better judgment. It also gave her a chance to pick up any supplies they needed.

Her mother normally took turns with her, but she had been ill and was too fragile to make the journey right now, especially with the rainy weather they had been experiencing recently. Lily had also stopped by the local sheriff's office to tell him what had happened. She was tired of them constantly having to look over their shoulders.

After the incident yesterday she was determined to end Butler's advances. She asked the sheriff if it would be possible for him to talk to Butler about staying away from them. The sheriff had explained he would talk to him, but suggested it might be a good idea if Lily and her mother found somewhere else to stay for a while. Lily had shaken her head; they had no other family. The farm was the only place they had.

The sheriff said he would be out the next day to talk with Maureen and see what he could do to help out. Lily had thanked him before making the long journey home. Now, as she struggled to get home before dark, she was suddenly filled with a sense of unease. Had she done the right thing? Would Butler become even more hostile? More determined?

Frowning as she made her way up onto the small porch, she realized there were no lights on in the small house. Opening the door, Lily pushed her wet hat off and laid it next to the door.

"Momma?" Lily called softly. "Are you here?"

Lily set the basket of supplies down on the rough table in the kitchen. Removing her wet jacket, she walked to the door of her mother's bedroom.

Hesitating, she knocked softly. "Momma?"

The door opened suddenly with a bang as it swung back and hit the wall. A very drunk James Butler stood in front of her wearing nothing but a pair of half-buttoned pants, with a bottle of whiskey in his hand. "Your momma ain't here no more, little girl. It's just you and me now."

Lily stepped back from the stench of bad breath and whiskey coming from the man standing in front of her. She looked around his large body into her mother's bedroom and saw her mother lying naked on the bed, her face bloodied and bruised, her eyes staring unseeing toward the ceiling. Lily's eyes grew wide in horror. Sobbing, she stumbled backward as Butler reached for her.

"You're gonna fill the bitch's position now, and I know just the position I want to take you in too." He grinned as he grabbed his crotch. "I've wanted to fuck you ever since I first laid eyes on you. I wanted your momma too, but she couldn't handle me. Bitch scratched my face up when I told her what I was gonna do to you. She knew I wanted you. I made sure I told her as I fucked her what I was going to do to her baby girl. I even let her know her beloved husband had a little help in meeting an early grave. He didn't know what hit him until it was too late. You and your momma always thought you were too good for me. Bet she didn't think that as she was getting fucked. She kept begging me. You know how much that turned me on? You should have listened to her beg me not to hurt you when I told her how I was gonna fuck you too."

Lily shook her head as she moved around the table, trying to keep away from the monster who had murdered her family. She shook with grief over what her beautiful and gentle mother had gone through.

"How could you?" Tears poured down her face as she realized she was about to meet the same fate as her mother. "How could you?"

Taking another swig of whiskey, James laughed as he threw the bottle at her across the table. "You should have heard her. Your momma begged for protection for you with her dying breath. 'Please give my baby girl a chance to live. Please, oh God, please, protect my baby girl.' I don't think anyone was listening, do you? No one heard her as she begged for her life." He whined out the words, noting how each one pierced the heart of the girl in front of him.

"Come here and bend over, girl. It's time I showed you what a man feels like. Maybe if you are a good girl I won't have to beat you like I did your momma. She shouldn't have fought me. She got what she deserved," James said as he began undoing the rest of the buttons on his pants.

Lily backed up until her back was against the edge of the counter. Screaming when James grabbed the table and flipped it out of the way, Lily reached blindly behind her for some type of weapon. Her hands closed around the small lantern they used in the kitchen.

She flung it at him with all her might, not waiting to see if it made contact. Turning, she rushed to the back door of the small house and stumbled down the steps, sobbing. She ignored everything but the need to get away, running as fast as she could in the driving rain.

She headed around the back, running across the muddy yard past the barn and down toward the river that ran along the back of the property. Her only thought was to get away from the evil that had taken her family away from her. If she could get to the next farm she would be safe, she kept telling herself over and over.

She screamed suddenly in fear when her long hair was grabbed painfully from behind, pulling her off her feet. She landed on her back in the thick mud and began tumbling down the slight incline toward the river fighting against the huge body trying to hold onto her.

Lily gasped as a fist came down along her chin. It hadn't been a hard blow, but enough to stun her for a moment. Her legs were tangled in the skirts of her long dress, and she couldn't seem to fight her way free of them long enough to get up.

When the muddy hand tightened its grip in her hair and began to drag her up to her knees, she screamed even louder in pain and fear. She frantically swung her fists as hard as she could in an effort to break free. She almost sobbed in relief when she connected, listening with satisfaction when she heard a grunt of pain over the rain and thunder. Pushing with all her might, she wiggled free from Bulter's muddy grasp and struggled to her feet. She stumbled blindly toward the rain-swollen river.

Lily gasped in dismay as she realized she would never be able to safely cross the river. The rains had swollen the it to over twice its normal size. The waters rushed in torrents, tearing away at the bank, twisting and churning in wild rapids of fast-moving water.

Turning in defeat, she wrapped her arms around her waist as she looked into the angry face of the man who had murdered her parents. She watched in despair as he moved toward her with a hateful grin on his muddy face. Straightening her shoulders, Lily spoke quietly.

"You won't get away with this. You'll receive justice for the murder of my family. The sheriff knows what you have been doing. He is coming out tomorrow to check on us. I told him about what you did yesterday. You are going to hang for murder."

"Who do you think he is going to believe when he doesn't find anything? He'll think you and your momma just up and left. If you want to talk about justice, girl, I'll show you justice. Justice is when I bury my dick deep inside your pussy just like I did your momma for thinking she was too good for me." James wiped the mud dripping down his face. "What are you gonna do now? You don't have anywhere else to run too. You're all out of choices."

"There is always a choice. You made yours, and I hope you rot in hell. If I'm going to die, I'll do it with the knowledge you will never do to me what you did to my mother," Lily replied with cold determination.

She raised her eyes briefly to the sky and let out a small prayer, seeking forgiveness for what she was about to do. Twirling around, she jumped off the eroding bank into the swiftly moving water. The dark, swirling waters closed over her head, the weight of her dress dragging her down deeper into her watery grave. Lily couldn't help but think how she hadn't even had a chance to live before she died and felt regret she would never know love the way her parents had.

* * *

"Caleb, you do something with him! I've had it," Ethan called out as he slammed his hat on his head and headed out the door. "I'll be back in two weeks."

Caleb just gritted his teeth as he slammed his own hat on his head and headed for the back door. He had enough to do without babysitting his goddamn brother. Allen had made his own bed, and nothing he or Ethan did seem to help.

"Maggie, can you see if you can get Allen to open the door long enough to bring him some decent food and maybe talk him into getting a bath? I've got to head to the western pasture to take care of a fencing issue. I won't be home for a couple of days, maybe more. I'll be staying at the old line shack in case you need me," Caleb asked before turning and walking away.

Maggie stood staring at the retreating figure of Caleb. Shaking her head, she went into the kitchen and made a ham, egg, and cheese sandwich for Allen. The boys were going to be the death of her. She was seventy-two years old and couldn't keep up with them anymore, especially since Allen came back home to live on the ranch.

Moving slowly through the living room to the downstairs guest bedroom Allen had taken over on his return, she carefully balanced the tray on her hip. Knocking softly, she opened the door to a darkened room when she received no reply. Frowning, she sniffed and shook her head.

The room stank of male body odor and stale whiskey. She moved carefully over to the small table in front of the window and set the tray down. Pulling back the curtains to let some light into the room, she jumped when a loud voice yelled out.

"Goddammit. Shut the fucking curtains. If I had wanted them open, I would have opened the damn things. Get the fuck out of my room," a harsh voice demanded.

Putting her hands on her aged hips, Maggie glared at the disheveled figure in the bed. Bare from the waist up, with a six-month growth of uncut beard covering his chin and dark curly hair covering his chest, Allen Cunnings was a scary figure.

At over six feet two he could be intimidating anyway. It was hard to tell this was the same handsome young man all the girls in town drooled over for years. His normally neatly trimmed light brown hair hung down past his shoulders and was matted from not having been washed or combed in God knew how long.

He still had the muscled chest from years of hard work, but he had lost a lot of weight and was too thin. Allen ignored Maggie's glare, rolling over to feel along the floor next to the bed. He grunted when his fingers wrapped around the top of a partial bottle of whiskey. He dragged it up and pulled the cork.

"Boy, it's eight o'clock in the morning. Don't you think that is a little early to be hitting the bottle? And you need a bath. You stink and so does this room. How do you stand it?"

"Just close the damn curtains and get out, Maggie. I'm a grown man and can do what I want," Allen growled. "Tell Ethan I need some more whiskey."

"Ethan is gone for the next two weeks at an auction in Texas," Maggie said as she moved to pick up some dirty clothes off the floor.

"Well, tell Caleb I need more, then," Allen demanded with a snarl.

"Caleb is gone to the western pasture and won't be back for several days."

"Will you just drop my damn clothes? I don't need a nursemaid. You go get me some more whiskey,"

Allen said, turning to take a deep swig out of the almost empty bottle.

Maggie dropped the clothes in frustration and glared at Allen; shaking her finger at him, she had finally had enough. "You don't need a nursemaid, remember? Get your own damn whiskey. I am through putting up with you and your brothers' bad tempers. You don't need a housekeeper; you need an angel who could put up with all the crap you boys have been giving everyone. I came to help out, but this is beyond me. I'm going to town and not coming back without a new housekeeper who can put up with all you boys' shit."

Maggie Cunnings had a spitfire of a temper when roused, and she was tired of putting up with all the clusterfucks her nephews had dished out. She had been coming back and forth to the ranch for the past two years, helping out between housekeepers. So far, the boys had driven off six housekeepers in the last six months, two of them men!

No one could put up with all the stuff the boys dished out. They weren't mean. No, they were just angry, confused, and ornery. None of them knew how to overcome what life had dished out to them.

Ethan was the oldest at thirty-three. He was trying to take on the responsibility of everyone. He had taken over the reins of the ranch when their parents had been killed in an airplane crash almost ten years before. He did all the bookkeeping, buying, and investments that made the ranch so profitable, as well as trying to be a ranch hand when needed. He was burning the candle at both ends and now felt responsible for what had happened to Allen.

Caleb bottled everything up, never letting anyone get too close to him. He spent as much time out on the range as he could. He made sure everything outside the house ran smoothly because he didn't know how to deal with what was happening inside it. He felt just as responsible for Allen being in the shape he was, believing he could have prevented what happened somehow. At thirty, he had always been the one to hold things in and not show much emotion. The problem was, it ate at the inside of him.

Allen, on the other hand, was angry at the world. He had taken off at twenty and joined the military against his older brothers' wishes, wanting to get away from the ranch. At twenty-eight, he had spent the last eight years traveling and fighting all over the world.

Eight months ago the boys' world crashed down around them when it was reported Allen was missing in action in South America. When he was finally rescued, he had been beaten and tortured. At first, it was unclear if he would even make it. Both his legs had been broken, and he was covered in cuts and bruises. The jungle climate had been perfect for infection to set in, and when he had been transported to the closest military hospital it had been touch and go for the next week.

The military doctors had reset his legs, and he was healing slowly. He no longer needed the wheelchair. Ethan and Caleb had brought him home six months ago, and he hadn't left the room they had set up for him since, preferring to hide in the dark with his whiskey.

Ethan and Caleb had tried at first to get him to go to physical therapy, only to have every therapist in a four-state region refuse to come back to the ranch, no matter how much they offered to pay them. As the pressure of everything going on increased, one housekeeper after another began leaving as the boys' tempers escalated to a breaking point.

They could hardly stand being together in the same room. Maggie had stepped in again two months ago, but even she was at her wit's end. The boys needed a miracle, and she needed to find it. Standing in the kitchen, she put on her coat and picked up her purse.

"Please, Lord, if you are listening, my boys need an angel, one with a lot of patience. If you can find one you can share, I'd be mighty appreciative. I know I don't talk to you as often as I should, but the boys need someone to love and who can love them. Please, if you can find the time, please send my boys an angel to love."

Sighing, she closed the door just as she heard a bottle crashing against a wall and a loud curse. Pulling her gloves on to ward off the cold Wyoming winter, she walked out to the truck and drove to town on a mission.

Chapter 2

Maggie pulled into the parking space in front of The Flats Grill. The old diner was a favorite among the locals. If you needed news or wanted to find someone to help you out, this was the place to go. Any news in Boulder Flats, Wyoming would pass through the diner at some point.

Getting out of the truck, Maggie felt every minute of her seventy-two years. She pushed open the door and moved to a booth near the back of the diner. She would ask Gladys if she knew of anyone looking for a housekeeping job. She would have to let whoever interviewed know it would be in a combat zone.

Dropping her scarf and purse on the seat next to her, she removed her heavy coat and hung it on the coat rack next to the corridor leading to the bathrooms. Sitting down heavily, she smiled when she saw Gladys coming with two cups of steaming coffee. Gladys' slim body and head of silver hair barely showed her seventy years as she moved with a spry step in her walk toward the booth. She carried the two cups with the experience of years of serving.

"Hey, Maggie," a pair of voices called out behind Gladys.

Carl and Earl Ganders were Glady's husbands. Tall and thin, they were still handsome as sin. In a time when it was considered unusual Gladys had fallen in love with the twin brothers, and they had fallen in love with her.

The men had advertised for brides, but only Gladys had arrived on the bus. They had taken one look at her, and knew she was it for both of them. They had recently celebrated their fiftieth wedding anniversary.

"The boys giving you fits again?" Gladys asked with a knowing smile, sliding into the seat across from Maggie.

There had been a lot of disgruntled ex-housekeepers flowing through the diner in recent months. She had heard all about some of the more colorful fights at the ranch, including Ethan and Caleb's attempt to hire a hooker for Allen. Seemed Caleb figured if Allen had sex he would be in a better mood, as it had helped in the past. He had talked Ethan into talking to a friend of a friend who knew a woman from Nevada who was willing to come in.

In the end, Allen had not been appreciative, and the woman had left in a huff—but not before threatening to tell the sheriff about what the brothers had tried to do if they didn't pay her a six-figure sum to keep quiet. Of course, the sheriff, Matt Holden—who was a childhood friend of the boys—had threatened to arrest the woman for blackmail and prostitution. According to the housekeeper at the time, the woman left with her promised two hundred and fifty dollars and a bus ticket out of town.

"I just don't know what to do. Ethan took off for two weeks on the excuse he needed to go to an auction. Caleb would rather spend a week out on the range in freezing weather than be in the house. And Allen—" Shaking her head, Maggie took a drink of the hot coffee before continuing. "The boy is going to drink himself to death if something isn't done. I can't do any more. I need a miracle, Gladys."

Gladys sat quietly, wishing she could help her friend out. She was at her wits' end too. She didn't know a single person who was willing to take on the Cunnings men, no matter how rich or good-looking they were.

Sighing, she reached over and placed a supportive hand over Maggie's as she shook her head in sympathy. "I wish I could help you out."

Maggie spent the next hour talking with Gladys and her husbands. She enjoyed their company and missed them since she had moved to Florida. If the weather in Wyoming wasn't so damn cold in the winter, she would have stayed just to be near them. Her old bones just couldn't seem to handle it any more, plus she had met a really nice widower with whom she enjoyed spending time.

Just as she was resigning herself to returning to the ranch empty-handed, the bell over the door chimed. Maggie looked up and inhaled a deep breath. Standing just inside the door was a young girl. She had on a thin patchwork jacket and was wearing a pair of faded jeans and scuffed-up boots. What caught Maggie's eye was the light streaming in behind her. She didn't know if it was the play of the light through the ice-coated window or what, but the girl looked like she had a halo around her head.

"Gladys, Earl, Carl—look behind you," Maggie whispered excitedly. "I believe my angel just walked into your diner."

All three of them turned as one to look at the new arrival. Their eyes widened as they noticed the play of light surrounding her.

* * *

Lily stood in the door of the diner biting her lower lip with uncertainty. She pushed a strand of dark hair behind her ear as she looked around. She didn't have much money, but she needed to get warm and find something to eat.

The diner was the first place she had seen when she had arrived in town. Walking over to one of the barstools at the counter, she lowered her canvas bag and sat on the stool. Earl walked around the counter to take her order, smiling a welcome as he handed Lily a worn menu.

Lily looked at the menu for a minute trying to decide. Her mouth watered at all the delicious selections. She had a hard time choosing what to order. It would have to be something very inexpensive. She finally settled for ordering a glass of water, no ice, and a cup of soup.

It was all she could afford until she found a job. She would ask the man behind the counter before she left if he knew of anyone who might be hiring locally. She would also have to find a place to stay tonight. She really didn't have enough money for a room.

She sighed. She'd better get as warm as she could now, because she had a feeling she was going to be very cold tonight if she couldn't find a really, really cheap place to sleep. Pulling out a small battered change purse, she pulled a couple of crumpled dollar bills out of it. She sighed again; she was going to have to find a job soon or she would be going hungry as well as cold.

Sipping the hot soup, she let the warmth slide through her frozen body. She hadn't realized it was so cold out until she came in out of it. Smiling at the man behind the counter, Lily asked softly. "You wouldn't know if anyone around could use a good housekeeper or cook do you? I'm a hard worker and dependable."

Gladys had risen when Lily had ordered, moving toward the kitchen. She smiled at Maggie as she walked by her. "This one is a keeper. I say hire her if she needs a job. She is just what the boys need," she whispered.

Maggie had been sitting in the booth watching the young girl as she looked over the menu. She could tell the girl was cold and hungry, but probably didn't have much money, if her jacket was any indication. It was hardly appropriate for early October in Wyoming.

When Maggie heard her ask Earl about a job, she thought she had hit pay dirt. She stood up and walked over to the girl. Maggie studied her closely for a minute before speaking.

"I might know someone who's looking for a housekeeper. My name's Maggie Cunnings. Why don't you sit down with me at the booth over there, and we'll talk for a bit?"

Lily studied the older woman for a moment before nodding. The woman looked to be in her late sixties or early seventies. It was hard to tell really, as she had one of those ageless faces.

Lily couldn't believe her luck. She watched wide-eyed as the woman turned and went back to the booth she had been sitting at when Lily had first come into the diner. Lily quickly collected her canvas bag and picked up her water. When she turned to grab her cup of soup, Carl had already picked it up and placed it on the table across from Maggie, along with a cup of hot tea.

She started to say she hadn't ordered hot tea, but her protest died when she saw Carl wink at her. Smiling her thanks, Lily turned to study the woman sitting across from her as she slid into the booth. Maggie continued to stare at her for a moment longer. Feeling a little self-conscious, Lily tucked a stray strand of her dark brown hair behind her ear.

"So, you want to be a housekeeper?" Maggie began.

"Yes, ma'am. My name is Lily. I have plenty of experience with maintaining a house, and I'm an excellent cook. I am also very good with children," Lily said earnestly. "I'm honest and dependable, too."

"Call me Maggie. I'm sure you are, dear. I can tell a lot from the way a person holds themselves if they are telling me the truth. The house you would be working at has three males in it. They are brothers. Ethan is the oldest, followed by Caleb and Allen. They aren't easy to work for, but they are good men. They've been through six housekeepers in the last eight months."

Lily leaned back and stared into Maggie's eyes thoughtfully. "If you ask me, it sounds like they haven't found the right person for the job yet. I'm not afraid of hard work, and it isn't easy to drive me off, ma'am. I stay until the job is done. Do you mind me asking if they are married? Do they have any children who need tending?"

Maggie smiled at the old-fashioned term. "None of them are married and none of them have children—at least none that we know of," Maggie said humorously. "It hasn't been easy. All three of those boys need a strong hand to get them into shape. I've done the best I can over the past two months, but I'm getting too old for this."

"Are you their housekeeper? Will they have a problem with you hiring me?" Lily asked curiously.

"I'm their aunt. I've been helping out. Each one of those boys needs something different. They all have very distinctive personalities. Ethan works too hard and never takes time for himself. Caleb bottles everything up, and it eats away at him. But the one needing the most help is Allen. He has a lot of anger he needs to work through. They have grown apart over the years and now can't seem to be around each other for very long without losing their tempers and fighting," Maggie said, watching carefully for Lily's reaction. She wondered if she was giving Lily too much information, information that would scare her off. Maggie let out a small prayer, hoping Lily would be strong enough to accept the challenge. She felt it was only right Lily knew all the facts going into the position.

Lily smiled gently. "It really sounds like they need more than a housekeeper. They need someone who can help them become a family again."

Maggie grinned with relief at Lily's insight. "You might be right. Those boys need someone who won't leave the first time they growl at them. They need to learn there is more to life than work or heartache. And, they need to learn how to be brothers again. They were very close growing up, always hanging out with each other and supporting one another through all the scrapes they used to get into. It seems like they have forgotten that."

Lily nodded. "Ma'am, Maggie, I need a job, and it sounds like your boys need an experienced housekeeper who won't take their growling personal. If you are willing to hire me, I won't disappoint you. I'll stay as long as they need me."

"Well, then, consider yourself hired! I need you to start as soon as possible. Are you staying in town? Can you start tonight?" Maggie couldn't contain her joy at the prospect of Lily being at the ranch. Somehow, she knew Lily was the right one. If Maggie didn't know any better she would have thought Lily had been heaven-sent as she fit her earlier prayer for an angel to help get those boys back in shape.

"Actually, I just got off the bus, and I haven't found a place to stay or anything yet. All I have is what's in my bag." Lily nodded to the large canvas bag at her feet. Lily didn't want to admit she didn't have any money to stay anywhere, and the thought of a nice warm bed was a welcome relief.

Maggie frowned, looking at Lily's jacket. "We need to get you a few things. Your jacket isn't going to help keep you warm. We'll head over to Pete's Trade Stop before heading out to the ranch. They'll have everything you'll need."

Lily shook her head, determination made her lips form a straight line. She never took anything without being able to pay for it. Her parents had raised her to believe it just wasn't right.

"I'll get it when I get my first paycheck. I have enough to keep me warm until then. I don't want to take anything until I've earned it."

Maggie studied the girl sitting across from her. She seemed so young, but her eyes told a different story. "Child, how old are you? Do your parents know where you are?"

Lily smiled sadly. "I'm older than I look. My parents passed away a few years ago, and I don't have any other family. I've been on my own for a while now," she explained in a quiet voice.

Maggie's eyes shone with compassion, "Well, let's get you out to the ranch. I can show you the house tonight, and if you don't mind, I'll head out back to town tonight so I can get an early start in the morning. I miss my Albert something fierce, not to mention the warm, sunny weather of south Florida. Albert and I met there ten years ago when I moved to get away from the cold Wyoming winters. I have to admit, I don't miss them at all."

Lily suddenly had a terrible thought. "Maggie, what if the men don't like me? What if they fire me before I even have a chance to prove myself?"

"Now, don't you mind those boys. I'm the one hiring you, so they can't fire you unless I tell them they can. In fact, I will guarantee you the first three months' salary plus living accommodations just for taking the job. How does that sound?"

Lily couldn't help the relieved smile that curved her lips. "Like a plan. You won't regret it, Maggie, I promise."

"Gladys, Carl, Earl, I've found a new housekeeper for the boys. I'm going to take her out to the ranch and get her settled in. If you don't mind, can I stay at your place tonight so I can head out early tomorrow morning for the airport? It will save me at least an hour's drive," Maggie asked as she gathered her things together.

Gladys smiled warmly at Lily before replying. "Anytime, Maggie. You know that. The guest room has your name on it." Maggie gave Gladys a quick kiss on the cheek and flushed when both Earl and Carl came up and gave her a kiss on the lips. Shaking her head at the two men, she turned and grinned at Lily, a nice pink glow on her cheeks.

Lily gathered her bag and waited as Maggie put on her coat and gloves. Following the older woman out the door, Lily turned at the last minute to look at Gladys, Carl, and Earl. "Thank you. The soup and hot tea were very good."

Gladys leaned back into Earl's arms and smiled up at both men. "I think those Cunnings men aren't going to know what hit them."

Carl leaned down and gave Gladys a kiss. "I think you're right, dear. I think you're right."

Earl tightened his hold on Gladys and smiled. "I think they have finally met their match. I just hope they are smart enough not to throw her away."

Chapter 3

It took almost an hour to get to the ranch house. Lily looked out the window of the truck, studying the white landscape dotted with evergreens. She loved the winter as much as she loved the other seasons. Each one had something special about it. In the spring the earth just seemed to come alive with new growth and new life. The summer was a time of sunshine and warmth, while the fall had all the colors of the earth mixed together. The winter, though, it was special in its own right.

The snow glistened like millions of diamonds scattered about and swirled with hidden colors only the sun could bring out. It was a time of warm fires, hot chocolate, and families being together. Sighing, she turned when Maggie started telling her about the ranch.

Lily listened carefully as Maggie explained how the ranch had been in the family for the past five generations with the first Cunnings coming out to settle the west by wagon train. They had stopped in Wyoming and settled. Since then, the ranch had grown and prospered over the years to encompass over a hundred thousand acres of wood, pasture, and cattle land.

The ranch had passed to the boys when their parents had passed away in a plane crash ten years before. Ethan had only been twenty-three, but he took over the reins of both the ranch and his younger brothers. Maggie was their aunt on their fathers' side and had never married. A few years after she had moved to Florida for the warmer climate, she had met a widower named Albert whom she "dated."

"Now, child, tell me a little about you," Maggie asked.

"There's really not much to tell. My parents died a few years back, and I have moved around working as a housekeeper. I never leave until I'm no longer needed, so you don't have to worry. One family I worked for just needed help until the mother had recovered from an illness. Another needed help with their young child. My last family needed help dealing with the death of one of the parents. Once the father remarried, I was no longer needed."

"How could they say you were no longer needed? Didn't they care about you? What about what you needed?" Maggie asked curiously.

"It's all right. I knew I wouldn't be in any of the homes for very long. A few months to a year is usually all it takes to get things back on track. I guess you can say I just stay until the family has healed. It's for the best. I like meeting new people, and this gives me the opportunity to travel and explore the world," Lily replied calmly.

She didn't need Maggie to know how much it hurt to leave the children she had grown attached to or to see the love develop between the couples she had helped to find their way. No, she accepted her time with each family as a precious gift. For just a little while, she would be a part of a family again. That was enough.

"Well, we're here. Now, don't mind Allen. He has a surly mouth on him, but he's all bark. You remember that," Maggie said as she pulled in front of the large two-story house.

Lily's breath caught in her throat as she stared at the beautiful home. The house had a huge wraparound porch and a double door leading into the it. On the porch were several rocking chairs and small tables. The front of the house had a large window overlooking the drive.

There was a large red barn over to the far left. Following Maggie as she got out of the truck, Lily grabbed her canvas bag and held it to her chest. Her eyes were wide with wonder as she followed Maggie up the steps and into the house.

Pausing in the doorway, she looked around the foyer. The house was an open design with a staircase curving up to the second floor. There was a balcony leading along the second floor that looked down into the spacious living room. On one wall was a huge fireplace, but no fire was lit in it. The back wall was nothing but windows looking out over the mountains. Maggie removed her coat and gloves, hanging it on the jacket rack inside the door.

"Upstairs are the main bedrooms. There are four upstairs and two downstairs. Ethan and Caleb each have a room upstairs. Allen's was upstairs, but since he came back, he has been using the downstairs guest room. There is also the master bedroom, but no one uses it yet. The other bedroom is off the kitchen and is for the housekeeper. That will be your room. I've been using it while I was here since I can't get up those stairs the way I used to. I'll throw the sheets in the washer before I go. There are more in the linen closet off the bathroom. There is a third floor, but it is just an open attic used for storage. The house has seven bathrooms. Guess they figured with all the boys they needed a bathroom for each one and plus extras for any guests. Each room has its own bathroom, so be prepared. I never did like cleaning the damn things. Downstairs there is the main living room, a family room off the kitchen on the east end of the house and the bedroom and office on the west side. There is also a den-slash-library. The basement access is through the kitchen, which also has a servant's entrance for upstairs. You'll find the washing machine and dryer down there as well as a sauna. Don't worry about having to lug everything up and down those stairs; luckily they have a laundry chute and dumb waiter to haul stuff up and down. The boys were forever getting in trouble when they were younger. Once Allen and Caleb got mad at Ethan for bossing them around and put him down the laundry chute. They had locked the end, though, and he couldn't get out. His mama found him an hour later. Thought she was gonna rip the hide off those two younger boys. Next day, Ethan stuffed both boys in the dumbwaiter and wouldn't let them out," she explained.

Lily laughed at the idea of the mischief the boys had gotten into. She could just imagine them horsing around. She couldn't wait to meet all three of them and wondered if they still had some of that mischievous behavior left in them.

"Let me show you around. The kitchen is this way." Lily followed Maggie around for the next hour learning where everything was and how everything was set up.

Maggie told her the boys usually ate breakfast around five thirty every morning, and she would pack a lunch for them if they weren't able to make it back during the day. Dinner was usually around six o'clock. Allen hadn't been eating much since he came home, and Maggie was concerned about his health.

"Allen was in the military. He was in South America on some mission, and it went bad. He was captured and tortured. By the time they got him out he was almost dead. He's been home for six months now and hardly ever leaves the downstairs bedroom. All his meals are taken to him and left."

"Why hasn't he left his room?" Lily asked curiously, her heart going out to a man she hadn't even met yet.

"His legs were broken pretty bad. The docs were able to patch him back up, and he can walk now, but it wasn't always easy for him, especially when he was tired. He refused to work with the physical therapists, so it has been a little harder on him. He's better now physically, but mentally… Now that's another story."

"Why did he refuse the help of the physical therapist?" Lily asked, wondering if there was something she was missing.

"Allen wasn't the only one captured. Two of his buddies were captured as well. They were beaten and tortured too. They weren't as lucky as Allen. They didn't make it out alive," Maggie said sadly. "One of the boys was from here. He went into the military at the same time as Allen. Allen feels responsible for his death. He feels like he was the one who talked him into joining. Now he just drinks to forget. He still has nightmares at night."

"Hasn't anyone tried to help him? Surely the military has someone who can help him deal with the grief and anger he is feeling." Lily couldn't begin to imagine how difficult it must have been to watch two friends die in such a horrible way.

"He won't let anyone in. Everyone they've sent has walked out. I don't know what else to do and neither do his brothers. We've all tried to help, but nothing seems to work." Maggie wiped a tear away as it coursed down her withered cheek. "I'm hoping maybe you can help him, help his brothers, learn to live again, but I'm afraid he will just drive you away too."

Lily stared out the windows at the mountains for a moment before replying. "Sometimes you have to face death before you can appreciate what it means to live." Turning to look at Maggie, Lily gazed into the older woman's eyes and said quietly, "He just needs someone to show him the way. Maybe he just needs to realize his brothers need him as much as he needs them."

Maggie grabbed Lily's hands and squeezed them gently. "If anyone can help those boys learn to live and love again, it's you. They need you, Lily. I don't understand how I know. I just do. They need you."

Lily smiled sadly at Maggie and nodded. She knew what her mission was here. She needed to help the three brothers understand that no matter what life threw at them, if they stuck together they could overcome any obstacle. It would take time, patience, and a gentle push to get them headed in the right direction, but at least she knew what needed to be done. That was the first step in the right direction.

Chapter 4

Early the next morning, Lily hummed as she finished cleaning the living room area. Maggie had done her best, but the house had been neglected for quite some time. Now, a lovely warm fire burned in the hearth with a neat stack of wood next to it.

She had gone out at first light to explore the barn area and had met some of the men who worked on the ranch. Introducing herself as the new housekeeper, she had invited the men inside to enjoy some biscuits and sausage gravy and coffee. Brad Edwards, Harold Baker, Clive Simmons, and Ed Hammond had all worked at the ranch for the past ten or more years. Brad and Harold worked with the horses, while Clive was the ranch foreman, and Ed worked on the equipment.

Lily listened as the men talked about the day-to-day activities on the ranch. They normally ate in the kitchen connected to the bunkhouse, although Ed and Clive each had a small cabin of their own nearby. Clive was married. Ed had never married, and both Brad and Harold volunteered to marry Lily right then and there after tasting her biscuits and gravy and coffee. Lily blushed at the two younger men's flirting.

She learned a lot from the men about the Cunnings. They were known for being hardworking and honest. Most of the men on the ranch had been with them five years or longer because they enjoyed working for them and respected them.

Although Allen had been gone a lot over the past eight years, he had come home frequently and worked side by side with the men no matter what the job. Ethan was known for helping out the men and townspeople. Clive talked about how one of his sons had gotten into trouble with some drugs and needed help. Ethan had made sure the boy had gotten into a clinic to help sober him up and gave him a job on the ranch during the summers when he was out of school.

Caleb worked as hard as any of the men. He had saved one of the ranch hands from drowning last summer after the man's truck had swerved to miss a deer and went right into the river. Caleb had come upon him right after the accident. The man had been trapped by the steering wheel, and the truck cab had been filling with water. Caleb had broken through the windshield and was able to pull the steering wheel back far enough for the man to get free.

It wasn't so much the big things the men said that gave Lily a better understanding of the men they worked for, it was the way they talked about them. She could tell they cared for and respected each of the brothers.

Lily worked most of the morning on the downstairs rooms. She avoided Allen's room for now. She still wasn't quite sure how she was going to handle him. So far there hadn't been any sound out of the room.

In the early afternoon she planned to strip all the beds upstairs and play with the laundry chute. She was going to have fun with it and couldn't wait to see how the dumbwaiter worked. Opening the curtains in the den, she gasped as she saw the floor-to-ceiling bookshelves lining the walls. She immediately fell in love with the room and knew this would become her favorite place to hide.

Smiling, she walked around the room, staring at the pictures on the antique tables and running her hands over the bindings of many of the books. There was one wall with windows set on each side of a pair of French doors leading out onto the covered back porch area. If she was still there during the spring and summer she would have to sit outside on the porch and read.

She worked in the room for almost an hour when she heard a noise against the wall. Recognizing it as the water turning on, Lily smiled wickedly. Now would be a good time to check out Allen's room— while he was in the shower. If she was lucky, she could clean most of the room before he finished.

Lily hurried down the hallway and stood outside Allen's door for a moment with her ear pressed against the door. Knocking softly, she cautiously opened the door to peek in when she didn't get an answer. Sure enough she saw a light under the door to what had to be the bathroom.

Hurrying inside the dark room, she left the door open to the hallway so she could start throwing things out. The first thing she noticed was the smell. The room definitely had a male odor that needed airing out.

Lily hurried toward the windows, and despite the frigid temperature outside, threw open the windows on each side of the bed. Pulling the heavy curtains to one side, she knew they would have to go. No more hiding.

Twirling around, Lily moved like a woman possessed as she stripped the bed of all its linens and threw them out into the hallway. She grabbed one of the pillowcases and began filling it with empty whiskey bottles.

The pillowcase landed with a thump on top of the linens she had thrown out. Next, she gathered up all the old dishes and piled them outside the door. She grabbed, yanked, and dragged everything she could get her hands on out the door as fast as she could. Close to an hour later she figured she had less than five minutes left to get as much as she could out of the room before Allen came out, judging from the sounds coming from the bathroom. She planned on charging into the bathroom as soon as he was out and locking herself in it to give herself time to clean it. Then she would move everything out of the hall and wash, dry, and toss.

She had just finished closing the door to the hallway when she heard him moving. She raced to stand just to the left of the bathroom door so he wouldn't see her right away. Holding her breath, she waited, trembling.

* * *

Allen felt bad about the way he had treated Maggie. He knew he needed to apologize to her; he just wasn't sure how to go about it. He felt like hell.

He had woken up with a hangover and was nauseated by his own body odor. He thought the least he could do was get cleaned up before he faced his aunt.

Groaning as he rolled over, he sat up and grabbed his aching head. He sat for a moment until the room quit spinning. Once the room was still, he waited a moment more until he could focus his eyes on the door to the bathroom. It was going to be a long trip. If he could make it there without throwing up, he might make it through the day after all.

Rising unsteadily to his feet, he grabbed the crutches next to the bed. He used them mostly to help him stay upright. Wobbling as he headed for the door, he let out a loud expletive when he ran into the doorframe. Dropping the crutches, he staggered to the counter, slamming the door to the bathroom closed with one hand and clutching the sink counter with the other.

Damn, but he felt like shit. Running a hand over his chin, he grimaced when he saw the shaggy beard covering his face. He rummaged around in the bathroom drawer until he found a pair of scissors. It was too long to just shave it, he would have to cut it first, then shave.

His hair wasn't much better. Hanging in matted locks from lying down so long and not washing it, he looked like a homeless man out of the movies. Shuddering at the sight, he couldn't help but wonder what he had become.

Maybe it would have been better if he *had* been killed in the damn jungle with his friends. Shaking his head fiercely from side to side, he almost landed on his ass as his head protested the movement. He took a deep breath, and raising a trembling hand, he began cutting off his beard. It took him a good thirty minutes to just shave, and his face featured a few new cuts.

Pulling away from the mirror, he turned the shower to the hottest setting and waited as the water warmed up. Stepping in, he flexed his shoulders as the warmth from the shower beat down on his sore muscles. He shampooed his hair twice and had to leave the conditioner on for an additional five minutes before he could even run his fingers through his hair.

He didn't get out of the shower until the water turned so cold he was shivering from the chill of it. He felt marginally better, and he was hungry, something he hadn't been for quite some time. He had lost almost forty pounds since his capture and return.

Stepping out of the shower, he grabbed a comb and worked it through his damp hair. He grinned as he thought of what his brothers would say when they saw his hair down past his shoulders. All three of them had always worn their hair short.

He kind of liked having it long and thought he might just keep it that way. Wrapping a towel around his slender waist, he moved slowly to the door. He was still a little shaky from not using his legs in a while. He knew he should be doing the exercises the physical therapists and doctors had prescribed, but he had sunk so low he just didn't give a damn about whether he lived or died, much less whether he ever walked again.

Opening the door to the bedroom his first thought was it was way too bright. Maggie must have come in while he was in the shower and opened the damn blinds again. The second thing he noticed was it was cold as hell in the room. He walked slowly toward one of the windows and noticed it was opened.

"Dammit, Maggie!" Allen yelled crossly. "You trying to freeze my ass out of the room now?"

He muttered a long list of expletives under his breath. He was so pissed at being cold, he didn't even look as he exited the bathroom. It wasn't until he heard the door to the bathroom close behind him that he turned.

The movement was too much for his under used legs and throbbing head. Allen fell across the bed with a thump and a curse. That was when he noticed all his bed linens were missing.

"Goddammit, Maggie. I told you to stay out of my room. Get the hell out of there and make my bed," Allen growled out in irritation.

"Maggie's not here. You'll have to wait until I've washed the linens before you can lie back down," a soft voice replied from behind the bathroom door. "Oh, and you better get dressed before I come out. I plan on washing that towel you are wearing whether you are dressed or not."

Allen stared in stunned silence at the door. "Who the hell are you?"

Lily opened the door to peek out. "Lily. I'm your new housekeeper. Now get dressed before you catch your death of a cold. Your room needed to be aired out." Lily wrinkled up her nose. "It was a bit on the smelly side." With that, she closed and locked the door to the bathroom again.

Allen couldn't help but stare at the face peering out from behind his bathroom door. Long, dark brown hair was piled up on top of her heart-shaped face. Dark, dark lashes outlined eyes the color of a Wyoming summer-blue sky. His gazed took in the small, pert nose and lush full lips. Lips he could almost taste from where he was lying.

She was wearing a white sweater with a deep V-neck. It showed off her slim waist and very full breasts. She wasn't very tall, maybe five feet four, but had curves in all the right places. Her long legs were encased in a pair of faded blue jeans, and her feet were bare except for a pair of thick, woolen socks.

He couldn't help but stare at her when she wrinkled up her nose. It reminded him of the witch from the old television series who used to wiggle her nose before she cast a spell. At that moment, Allen felt like he had just been spelled by the most beautiful little witch he had ever set eyes on.

For a moment, their eyes met, then hers grew larger before her face turned a delicate pink, and she shut and locked the bathroom door. It wasn't until then that Allen realized he had grown hard while looking at her, and the towel now stood tented in the front, emphasized by him lying sprawled across the bed.

"What does she expect? Barging into my room. Taking over my bathroom. Thrusting those lush boobs at me? Does she expect me to be a damn saint?" Cursing under his breath, he sat up and tried to adjust his wayward cock.

He managed to finally get control of his enthusiastic dick long enough to struggle into a pair of jeans. Pulling on a thick sweater, he marched over to the windows and slammed them shut. He was lucky his balls hadn't frozen. It had to be forty degrees in his room. Walking over to the bathroom door, he slammed his fist against it.

"Time to come out, baby doll. You need to get your ass back to town. You're fired," Allen called out as he raised his fist to bang on the door again, only to stumble forward when it opened first.

Lily ducked under the upturned arm pounding on the door and made for the bedroom door, her arms full of dirty clothes. She paused just long enough to grab the towel Allen had been wearing when he came out of the bathroom. Turning to look over her shoulder, she calmly looked him over from head to toe before replying.

"You didn't hire me, so you can't fire me. Besides, I have a contract guaranteeing me three months employment with living accommodations before I can be dismissed. Lunch will be on the table in the kitchen in thirty minutes. I suggest you be on time," she said as she pulled the door open. She caught it again with her foot to close it, shutting out any response Allen would have made.

Lily was shaking as she headed for the laundry chute between the bedroom and the kitchen. She started shoving dirty clothes into it as fast as she could. She even stuffed the pillowcase filled with empty bottles down the chute. She could sort everything out once she was down in the basement.

Having cleared the mess in the hallway, she headed for the kitchen with the dirty dishes from the bedroom. She dumped the dirty dishes in the sink before turning to get lunch ready. Grabbing sandwich fixings, she pulled the roast beef she had been cooking out of the oven and sliced it up for hot roast beef sandwiches. She set out some potato salad and ice tea.

Even though it was cold outside, she figured it was nice and warm inside, all except for Allen's room. She would build a fire in the fireplace when she made up his bed. She was bent over halfway in the refrigerator when she felt hands grab her from behind. Letting out a small scream, she hit her head on the shelf.

"Ouch!" Turning, she shut the door to the refrigerator and glared at Allen. "What do you think you are doing? You scared the daylights out of me!"

Allen hadn't known what to say to Lily when she had made her little comment about not being able to fire her. It had taken him a few minutes to locate his socks and shoes before he had walked stiffly out of his room and headed toward the kitchen.

When he had entered the kitchen the last thing he was expecting was to see her lush ass sticking up in the air, begging him to move behind her. His wayward cock had sprung to attention again, and even if his jeans did fit a lot looser than they had before, it was still painful. It had been a year since he had last had sex, and his cock was telling him it was wide awake, ready, and willing.

Allen thought about all the questions he wanted to ask the little spitfire staring up at him, but every sane thought vanished out of his head when he caught a whiff of her. She smelled like spring flowers and chocolate chip cookies all rolled into one. Bracing his arms on each side of her head, he leaned in, staring down into her dark blue eyes.

For a moment, he felt like he was free-falling. His gaze moved to her lips, and he couldn't control the way his body jerked when she ran her tongue over her lips to moisten them. He had to taste her. He felt wild with the need to crush her to him and make her his.

Lily watched as Allen's eyes glazed over. Frowning, she worried he was about to pass out on her. If he fell on her, she would be squished!

"Well, would you look at that!" she said hurriedly, looking behind Allen.

Allen turned. By God, if his aunt was behind him he was going to let her have it. He wasn't sure if he was going to light into her for distracting him from the kiss he was going to take or for bringing the sexy pixie into the house. Not seeing anyone, he turned around to find Lily gone. Looking under his arm, he frowned as he watched the backside of her disappear around the table out of his reach.

Lily took advantage of his distraction to duck under his arm and move around the table, setting out plates and cups. She needed to put some space between them. The man was positively lethal in close quarters.

"What?" Allen demanded, frustrated at Lily getting away from him again.

He wanted a kiss. He needed a kiss. He was going to get a kiss before she walked out of his life if it was the last thing he ever did. That was, if he could catch her long enough.

Dammit, Allen thought crossly, *I want more than a kiss.* He wanted to taste her so bad he felt like he was going to explode if he didn't. *Here I am, hard as a rock, and she is busy playing Susie Homemaker.*

He ground his teeth together in frustration. She was acting like she was totally blind to the effect she was having on him. So help him, if his brothers had put her up to this, he was going to kill them—after he fucked her first, though.

"Why, it's almost time for the men to come in," Lily replied with a cheerful smile, ignoring the glares he was sending her way. "You might want to sit down before you fall down. You look a little flushed."

Leaning over the table, she gave Allen another eyeful of cleavage. "Here, take a plate and start building yourself a sandwich. I don't expect there to be much left once the guys come in."

Allen looked down blankly at the plate she had thrust at him. "What about you? Aren't you going to eat?"

Lily laughed. "No, I'm full from taste-testing everything. The joys of cooking are you get to taste everything first to make sure it is edible. The consequence of that is you get full and don't want to eat when it is done. I have some things I want to get done. Oh, here they come. They'll keep you company."

Allen could only watch as the ball of energy who had swept him off his feet less than an hour ago swept from the room and down the stairs singing an old tune. He still never had a chance to ask if his brothers had sent her.

"Hey, boss man. Good to see you up and about," Clive said as he came in through the back door. He took off his hat and hung it on the hat rack next to the door.

"Hey, boss," Harold and Brad said in unison. Rubbing their hands together, they both had big grins on their faces.

"Where's Lily?" Brad asked. "Boy, this sure smells good. I swear I'm gonna marry the girl."

"You just met her this morning. How'd you know she is the one you want to marry?" Ed said in his deep, surly voice. Taking a bite of the sandwich he had made, he groaned. "Forget it, boy. I'm thinking she might appreciate an older man. One who can appreciate her fine cooking."

Allen listened to the banter going back and forth about who was going to marry Lily. The only one who didn't say much was Clive, probably because he was the only married one of the lot.

"I'm gonna ask her out. Just to let you guys know," Harold said. "She is the prettiest little thing I've seen in these parts in a while."

Allen slammed his cup down on the table, glaring at Brad and Harold. "No one will be asking Lily out or to get married or anything else. Where in the hell did she come from? Did Ethan and Caleb send for her?"

All the men stopped eating long enough to look at Allen. Brad asked curiously. "Why not, boss? You never minded before."

Clive cleared his throat before answering Allen. "Naw, your brothers don't even know about her. Maggie hired her after they left. Guess she met Lily in town last night and hired her. Maggie told me she guaranteed Lily three months living accommodations and salary. Maggie also told me to tell you not to scare Lily off 'cause she wasn't coming back until winter was over because it's too damn cold here for her."

"Yeah, boss. Ethan and Caleb didn't send for her. Maggie hired her. So why can't we ask her out?" Harold asked. "None of you minded before as long as we kept it after hours."

It was true some of the men had dated previous housekeepers. This part of Wyoming wasn't known for having a surplus of females, and the brothers had never put limits on the men's personal activities as long as it didn't affect what they did on the ranch.

In the contracts the employees signed, there was a sexual harassment clause that was carefully reviewed, and the brothers let any man, or woman, know sexual harassment would not be tolerated. At the same time, they could not say no if two consenting adults wanted to spend time together outside of work.

None of the brothers had ever had a desire to date one of their employees before. It was just common sense as it opened them up to repercussions. But Allen wasn't thinking about repercussions right now; all he could think about was the pretty little brunette downstairs in the basement. How did he explain to them he wanted her for himself and would kill any man who touched her without sounding crazy?

Unable to think of a rational response, Allen glared at Harold and reiterated, "Lily is off-limits."

The look he gave the men brooked no more discussion on the subject, and soon talk turned to what was going on around the ranch. Allen had forgotten how much he missed ranch life. He listened as the men talked about the new bulls Ethan had purchased for breeding, the expectations for the spring count, and the problems they had been having on the western side of the ranch with someone cutting the fences.

They were missing some cattle, but it hadn't been too big a deal yet. Caleb had taken one of the trucks and his horse, Buck, out and was staying in the old line shack to see if he could track what was happening.

Throughout the discussion, Allen's mind kept turning to the beautiful brunette with her tantalizing lips, big blue eyes, and perky nose that twitched. Shifting in his seat to try to relieve the pressure in the front of his jeans he seemed to get every time he thought of her, he wondered again what she would taste like.

* * *

Lily listened for a while on the stairwell near the kitchen door leading to the basement. She couldn't help but smile. This was the first step with Allen.

She had wanted to get him out of his room. She knew if it was too cold to stay in it, he would have to leave. The second step was to get him to eat some hot food with some good company.

She could hear the interest in his voice as he asked questions about the ranch. She even heard a chuckle when Harold and Brad related some of the antics the new horses were getting into. Seems there was one horse who loved to steal food from another and another who liked to steal the blankets hanging around.

She moved down the stairs to get the laundry going. She smiled sadly when she saw the number of empty whiskey bottles. The smell was almost overwhelming. For a moment she was lost in another time when the smell of whiskey had been overwhelming.

Brushing a stray tear, she carefully placed every bottle in the trash can. She walked up the basement stairs, coming to the butler's corridor leading to the kitchen and took the back stairs up to the second level. She still needed to clean the upstairs. She also wanted to spend some time exploring.

Allen wasn't the only one who needed help according to Maggie. Lily had already learned a lot about the men, but she felt she could learn even more from their personal space. There were four bedrooms on this floor.

She walked into the first room and knew immediately it had to have been Allen's. A huge king-size bed took up the center of the room. It was made from rich oak and stained a natural color. Along one wall there were pictures of his family hanging in a collage. She walked over to the wall and looked at them. There were pictures of him at different ages along with his brothers and his parents. Lily smiled when she saw the two tall men standing behind a beautiful woman in one picture. She saw the resemblance to Allen in one of the men. Moving from picture to picture, she could see the love shining through. There wasn't much left in the room, a couple of nightstands and a tall chest of drawers.

Opening a door, Lily discovered a closet filled with shirts and jeans. The upper shelf contained a few cowboy hats, and there were several pairs of boots on the floor. Closing the door, she walked to the other side of the room and found a huge bathroom. It contained a sunken Jacuzzi and a shower almost as big as his closet with two shower heads in it.

Obviously, big men needed big bathrooms, she thought with a grin. There was one huge window facing the mountains. Lily stood for a moment just enjoying the view before she realized she had better get busy if she didn't want to really get fired.

The room didn't take long to put in order since no one was staying in it. She quickly moved to the next room and decided it must belong to Caleb. It also had a king-size bed, but the furniture was much darker.

His room had a huge window as well. Caleb only had a couple of pictures, one of him and his brothers and one of his parents. She lightly ran her fingers over the picture. She had never imagined it possible to have not one, but two dads. His closet wasn't as neat as Allen's. Clothes were piled along the narrow shelves, and a few were scattered on the floor. It looked like he had just tossed his boots in without looking.

Shaking her head, she gathered up the clothes on the floor for washing and matched all the boots up neatly. Next, she turned to strip the bed. A shiver ran down her spine as she inhaled the masculine scent.

Unable to resist, she buried her face briefly in his pillow. Something strange stirred in her... almost like a need. She had felt the same thing when Allen had trapped her in the kitchen. She had never thought of herself as a woman with needs. Oh, she had wanted a family, but realized it was not to be. She had never reacted to any other man she had met, much less two of them. Glancing at the picture of Caleb's parents, she couldn't help but let a wishful sigh escape her lips. If only…

The bathroom was identical to Allen's in layout but with different colors and was much more lived in. There was shaving cream and his razor lying on the counter. A toothbrush and toothpaste were set in a holder, and a comb was next to the sink.

Lily spent a little longer cleaning Caleb's room, wondering what he would be like when she met him. Maggie had said he bottled things up. She would have to work on his being able to talk. She was an excellent listener.

The next room was definitely Ethan's. Everything was immaculate. The bed was made, and there wasn't a thing on the floor. The window covers were pulled back and tied neatly. A look in his closet had Lily laughing; even she wasn't that organized! The bathroom was also spotless.

Ethan must have cleaned it before he left. Unable to resist knowing what Ethan's scent would be, Lily walked over to a shirt hanging on a hanger next to the bathroom door and pulled it toward her. Inhaling deeply, the rich masculine scent of wood and soap filled her.

Closing her eyes, she was unprepared for the feelings rushing through her. She felt her womb clench, and something she had never felt before tightened even lower. Gasping, she released the shirt and hurried from the room. There was nothing to clean, and far too much danger in staying.

Lily made her way to the last room and slowly opened the door, not really knowing what to expect. The room was gigantic! A bed twice as big as the ones in the other rooms stood in the center. It was a huge four-posted bed. There were two mirrored dressers and two tall chests of drawers.

Walking to one of the doors, Lily discovered a huge walk-in closet. It was empty. Closing the door, she walked over to see if the bathroom was as big, or bigger, than the other bathrooms. She walked in and gasped as she studied it. There were mirrors everywhere.

A tub the size of a small pool sat in the center of the room. Along one wall was a huge shower. It looked like the water fell from the ceiling above it like rain. The counter containing the sink actually had three sinks. The last wall had huge windows looking out over the mountains, so if you were in the tub you could look out.

She didn't think she would ever get out of the tub if she got into it. The bathroom was clean, and she could tell it wasn't being used. This had to be the master bedroom.

"This was my parents' room." A quiet voice spoke behind Lily, making her jump.

Lily twirled around, a hand going to her throat. "Oh. You are very good at that, you know."

"At what?" Allen asked huskily.

He had been watching Lily for several minutes from the doorway. He enjoyed watching her framed against the windows overlooking the mountains he loved so much. He could picture her naked in the tub with her long hair unbraided and hanging down to her waist, her naked body reflected in all the mirrors. He had grown hard just thinking about it.

"Sneaking up on me and scaring me!" Lily said with a teasing smile before turning to look out the windows again. "Isn't it beautiful? I could live in this room alone."

Allen came up behind Lily unable to resist the desire to touch her. "Yes, absolutely beautiful," he murmured softly.

Allen closed his eyes for a moment as Lily's arousing scent swept through his body, nearly overwhelming him. He clenched his fists close to his sides in an effort to stop himself from dragging her down to the floor and taking her right there.

"Oh, well. This isn't getting the house clean," Lily said nervously as she moved a step away. "Why don't you go out and see the new horses? Harold and Brad said they would take me out riding. I told them I'd go in a few days after I got settled in and knew my way around the house a little better. I'm really excited. I haven't been riding in years." Lily started to move around Allen, but he reached out, wrapping his large hand around her arm to stop her from leaving.

"I'll take you riding," Allen growled softly. "I don't want you around those two."

Lily looked into Allen's dark brown eyes. For a moment she lost herself in a dream, a dream she knew could never exist for her. With a sad smile, she reached up with her free hand and laid it against Allen's cheek.

"You don't have to worry about them. I'm not interested in developing a relationship with anyone. That's not what I'm here for," she said quietly.

"What are you here for, Lily?" Allen whispered.

"To be your housekeeper as long as you need me." Lily dropped her hand and pulled away from Allen, heading out the door. "Now, if I don't want to lose my job I'd better get dinner going, or you'll have grounds to dismiss me."

Allen watched as Lily walked out of the door. She didn't hear Allen murmur softly. "Never, Lily. I have a feeling I'm always going to need you."

The next few days fell into a pattern of Allen getting up early and having breakfast with Lily and some of the other men. Harold and Brad were always in attendance during meals, much to Allen's aggravation. They didn't say anything flirty to Lily, but Allen grew more and more restless as he watched them watching her as she moved around the kitchen or laughed at something someone said.

He didn't like the way they stared at her ass when she bent over to get something out of the oven or refrigerator. He definitely didn't like the way they stared at her breasts like they were imagining feasting on them instead of the food she had just set in front of them. He could tell they were impatient to get her alone. He also knew if they ever did, he would beat the bloody hell out of them both.

After breakfast, Lily would chase him outside on the pretense of having him check on the chickens for her or to go see a new horse or some other excuse. Lunch was the same, but the evenings were his favorite.

He discovered Lily loved to hide in the den curled up with a good book. She loved to read, and after the second night—when he had discovered her in there—she had started reading to him. He loved to sit and listen to her.

It had been a little over a week since she had come, and he realized he hadn't had or wanted a drink. What amazed him even more was that he hadn't had any nightmares since she arrived. This was a first for him in over eight months.

Some evenings they would just talk, or more like, he would talk. Lily was always asking him questions about the ranch: what it was like when he was growing up, how the ranch had changed over the years, what his parents and brothers were like. The questions were never ending. He fell asleep each night thinking about her and woke excited at the idea of seeing her.

Chapter 5

"Hey, boss man," Ed said as he pulled up outside the line shack.

It had been a rough drive even for the four-wheel-drive pickup, but he knew Caleb had to be running low on supplies. Pulling a box of canned goods out of the passenger seat, he made his way toward the open door. Caleb nodded as Ed walked through. "When you coming home?"

"Depends on what you brought," Caleb said, turning away to throw another log in the old wood stove. "Why do you ask?"

Ed shrugged. "Just thought you would prefer some of your new housekeeper's good home cooking instead of this canned stuff. She sent you a present."

Caleb frowned. "What new housekeeper? Where's Maggie?" Caleb took the small cooler from Ed. Opening it, he was almost knocked over by the delicious smells coming from it. "Shit. What did she fix? This smells like heaven," Caleb said as his stomach growled noisily.

Pulling out three containers, he opened one to find a thick beef stew, the next one had corn bread, and the last had a big pile of brownies. He could barely contain the drool from dripping down his chin. He was sick to death of canned soup and beans.

Pulling a big spoon out of the bottom of the cooler, he took a bite of the still hot stew, groaning as it hit his taste buds. "Damn, but that's good."

Ed smiled. "Yeah, Lily is a damn good cook. Her chocolate chip cookies should be outlawed. She's fattening Allen up pretty good. Haven't seen the boy eat so much in years."

Caleb's head jerked up in surprise. "Allen's eating?"

"Yeah. Even he couldn't resist Lily's famous hot roast beef sandwiches. He's been working with Harold and Brad with some of the new horses we got in too. They can't do much with the weather outside, so they have the big barn set up for training the horses commands and stuff. Lily keeps him pretty busy around the house fixing things too."

"Who the hell is Lily, who hired her, and when did she start?" Caleb asked around a mouthful of corn bread. Damn, it even had butter melted in it the way he liked.

"Lily's the new housekeeper Maggie hired before she headed back to Florida a little over a week ago. She runs a tight ship and doesn't let Allen get away with much. Heard she threatened him with the back side of a broom if he didn't get out from under her feet yesterday. Never thought I'd see Allen move so fast again. I guess the threat of a mouthful of broom bristles was enough, though," Ed said before snatching one of the warm brownies off the plate.

Caleb bit back a growl. Those were his damn brownies, and he wasn't sharing. Hell, it had been years since he had had any. Pulling the plate closer, he shot a warning glare at Ed.

"You find anything while you were up here?" Ed asked with a grin.

"Found some tracks, but the snow keeps covering them up. It looks like they are coming in from the National Forest." Caleb's eyes closed as he sank his teeth into the warm brownie. Oh, hell, that was heaven. He looked across at Ed and wondered why he had a shit-eating grin on his face.

"Well, guess I'd better be getting back. Lily was making chocolate peanut butter pies for dessert tonight and oven-roasted chicken with all the fixings. I don't want to miss it." Ed stood up, put his hat on and pulled out his gloves. "When you planning on coming back to the homestead? Just in case Allen asks."

"Today. I'll be home before it gets dark," Caleb said gruffly.

He was ready for a hot shower, a soft bed, and more of the delicious food he had just eaten. Hell, he might even kiss the new housekeeper if her pies were as good as the brownies. He didn't give a damn what she looked like.

Ed just nodded before heading out to the truck. Caleb didn't see the grin spread across the old man's face.

Caleb shut the door of the shack and looked around the small, dingy interior. Yeah, he was ready for his own bed. Pulling out his duffle bag, he stuffed the few clothes he had brought with him into it.

He put the canned goods in the cabinets and put out the fire in the old wood stove. He made sure everything was secure and neat before he walked out to the pickup truck. He threw his few belongs in the front seat and started the engine to warm it up. Backing up the truck to the horse trailer, he hitched it, then went into the small lean-to containing two stalls.

Opening it, he led his horse, Buck, out. "Let's go home, boy. You can sleep in a nice warm barn tonight." The gelding flicked his tail back and forth and nodded his head up and down like he was agreeing with the idea.

Caleb munched on brownies on the drive home. He was worried about how Allen was doing. From what he could gather from Ed, Allen was actually out of his room and moving around. How the new housekeeper had accomplished such a miracle in less than a week when he, Ethan, and Maggie had been trying for six months was beyond him.

He wiped a few crumbs from the beard on his face. Grimacing, he couldn't wait to get a hot shower and a shave. He had never liked having hair on his face.

He grinned when he thought about Allen. Hell, he looked like Grizzly Adams. Personally, the stuff made him itch. He wondered if Allen had shaved yet and gotten a haircut. He was beginning to look like a damn castaway.

He pulled in front of the barn two hours later. He had to go slow pulling the trailer, and even then it had been hazardous. He slid out of the truck and walked around the back to unload Buck at the same time Brad came out of the barn.

"Hey, boss man. Welcome back. I'll take care of Buck and the truck and trailer for you if you want." Brad had already undone the back gate of the trailer and was walking Buck backward out of it.

"Thanks. I could use a hot shower and a shave," Caleb said, pulling his duffle bag out of the front seat.

"Just be sure to take your boots off before you track through the house. Lily will open a can of whip ass on you if you muddy up her floors. Last night she clobbered Harold in the ass with a wet mop when he forgot," Brad said with a big grin.

Caleb raised his hand in acknowledgement before he headed toward the back door and kitchen entrance. Dropping his duffle bag by the door to the basement, he went up the back stairs heading for his room. He paused outside of Allen's room when he heard laughing. Moving closer, he pressed his ear to the door.

"Come here, you little rascal. You are going to be in so much trouble," a soft, sexy, feminine voice said. "Oh, you are such a bad boy."

Caleb could barely suppress a groan. It had been over a year since he'd had sex, and now his brother was doing it in the middle of the day. Hell, if he had known Allen was going to rebound so well he wouldn't have wasted his energy on worrying about him.

Pushing away from the door, he hurried to his room and a hot shower. Shit, he better make it a cold one instead with the hard-on he had in his pants. He wondered if Allen's friend would be interested in a threesome. For the first time, he was actually interested in someone Allen was, at least if the voice that had given him the hard-on was any indication.

It had always been their hope they would find a woman who would want to be with them, all three of them. So far, it had remained a fruitless dream. It seemed his, Ethan's, and Allen's tastes in women differed dramatically. Ethan like the tall, willowy type; Allen liked the biker babes. And him, well, he wanted a country girl with an edge. What did they say? A lady outside the bedroom, but a whore in it.

Sighing, Caleb finished shaving and showering. As he dressed, he wondered if Allen and his lady friend were done. He would like to catch a glimpse of her to see if the sight of her affected him as bad as her voice did.

* * *

Lily was just putting the finishing touches on Allen's bedroom. Allen and Clive had gone into town earlier, and she wanted to be done before Allen returned. She had wanted to surprise him by getting it ready for him. He belonged back in his old room.

She had washed and cleaned everything. She had had a little help which was why it took a little longer than she expected. When she had gone out to the barn early this morning she had heard a little meowing sound coming from behind the chicken coup. She had found a little kitten about six weeks old shivering in the cold.

Unable to resist, she had scooped the little kitten up into her arms and carried him in with her. She had bathed him and snuggled him close into her jacket. Later she brought him upstairs with her and closed the door to Allen's room so he wouldn't get out. She couldn't help but laugh as he ran, played, and explored everything in the bedroom while she cleaned.

Now, she stood back and smiled. It was ready. She had made a few changes, adding a few personal touches: a couple of throw pillows on the bed, a book they had enjoyed together on the nightstand, fresh flowers she had picked up yesterday at the grocery store in a vase on the dresser.

"Come here, you little bugger," Lily called, scooping the kitten into her arms and snuggling with him before sliding him inside her jacket again. "Now, you be quiet. I don't know how the men will feel about having another little man in the house with them."

Lily had her head down and wasn't looking where she was going as she opened the bedroom door. She was more concerned with the little kitten snuggling up to her, so it was a surprise when she ran right into a pair of hard, muscular arms and a broad chest.

"Oh, I'm so sorry. I should have been watching where I was going," Lily exclaimed, startled.

She looked up into the darkest eyes she had ever seen. They were like melted dark chocolate. She sighed. She loved dark chocolate, she thought wistfully.

Caleb couldn't resist listening at the door to see if his brother was finished horsing around. The last thing he had expected was to feel the soft, warm, sweet-smelling body of a woman coming out of the room, straight into his arms.

Looking down, he was mesmerized by the deepest, bluest eyes, he had ever seen. His arms tightened automatically when he felt her trying to move away. He was lost in a haze of desire that was almost overwhelming.

Lily wiggled, trying to put some distance between them. Blushing a bright pink when she felt the hard bulge in the front of his pants, Lily nervously licked her lips whispering, "Uh, you can let go of me. I'm sorry for running into you." Glancing at the door of the bedroom to make sure it was closed all the way, Lily pulled away from the man holding her and backpedaled until she was far enough away to hurry down the front staircase. "I have to go."

Lily was blushing furiously as she hurried down the stairs. Oh my, she thought, she hadn't realized Caleb was so—everything. She had seen pictures of him on the walls in Allen's room. They had not done him justice. He was over six and a half feet of pure male. His black hair and dark chocolate eyes were enough to cause any woman's pulse to increase. Add to that his firm lips, hard muscles… and his scent!

It was far more powerful than when she had cradled his pillow to her. She could feel the heat burning between her legs at the thought of being wrapped in his arms again. Wow, was all Lily could think as she hurried to turn off the timer in the kitchen. She moved into her bedroom off the kitchen and pulled the sleeping kitten out of her jacket and laid him on a small blanket she had found in the basement.

"Now, you be a good boy and sleep while I finish up dinner. Afterwards, I'll come play with you some more." Lily kissed the top of the kitten's head. She gently closed the door to her bedroom.

Pulling on a pair of oven mitts, she set the roasted chicken on the top of the stove to cool a little and put in a big pan of yeast rolls. She expected Allen and Clive should be back any time. Clive was supposed to pick up his wife and bring her to dinner tonight, which was why Lily had set the dining-room table for dinner tonight instead of the kitchen table where they normally ate.

She had just enough time to start the wash for the dirty clothes Caleb had brought back before the men came in. She had almost tripped over it when she had come into the kitchen. Humming softly, she grabbed the bag and headed down the stairs.

* * *

Caleb stared in disbelief as the most beautiful woman he had ever met hurried down the front staircase. Glaring at his brother's door, he didn't know if he should bang on the door until Allen answered who the hell she was or ask him if he was crazy for letting her out of his sight, or if he should consider her fair game and go after her.

He made up his mind. He didn't care what she was to his brother after a moment. He was staking his claim on her. Now all he needed to do was find out where she had run off to.

He searched the kitchen and living room first, looking for her. Going down the hallway, he checked the office and den, letting out a frustrated expletive when he didn't find her. He was heading toward the living room and front door when he saw his brother coming down the stairs.

"Hey, you are home. I saw your truck outside and was looking for you," Allen said with a grin.

Caleb looked at his brother like he had never seen him before. If he hadn't known any better he would swear it was a different man standing in front of him. Gone was the long shaggy beard and matted hair. Gone were the glazed eyes from the whiskey and the mouth tight with anger. The biggest thing Caleb noticed that was missing was the haunted look in Allen's eyes. He could see the little brother he had grown up with.

"Yeah, I'm home," Caleb grunted past his shock. "Where is she?"

"Where's who?" Allen asked, watching Caleb with a wary expression.

"The girl you were banging upstairs," Caleb replied impatiently. He didn't want to take a chance of the girl disappearing for good.

"I wasn't banging any girl upstairs. I just got back from town with Clive," Allen replied, a confused expression crossing his face. "What the hell are you talking about?"

"I heard you two doing it earlier, and she was coming out of your bedroom upstairs just a few minutes ago. She sounded like she was having a whole hell of a lot of fun. She even commented on you being one very bad boy." Caleb almost growled at his brother. Just remembering her sexy laughter was enough to make him hard.

"What did she look like?" Allen asked with a sinking feeling.

He had left Brad and Harold here alone with Lily. Surely they wouldn't have been brazen enough to use his old bedroom to— He had a hard time even thinking it. Aw, hell no, he thought with growing rage.

"She was the prettiest damn thing I ever saw. Eyes the color of a summer sky, long dark brown hair you could wrap your fists around, and breasts the size of—" Caleb paused when he looked at the expression on his brother's face. He had never seen him this pissed off, even when he was drunk.

Allen could feel his face freezing as Caleb described Lily. He was going to kill Harold and Brad. He had told those sons of bitches to stay away from Lily. She was his. Lock, stock, and barrel. Hell, he hadn't even kissed her yet. All he had done was fantasize about it night after night and half the damn day. Shit, just the thought of them banging her was enough to make him crazy.

"Lily!" Allen roared furiously. "Lily, get your ass out here. Now, dammit!"

Lily had finished putting the dirty clothes on to wash in the basement and returned to the kitchen, where she was taking the dinner rolls out of the oven when she heard Allen yelling. She set the hot rolls on a folded dish towel and pulled off her oven mitts.

"Allen, you owe me fifty cents. You said two bad words. Pay up," Lily said as she walked into the living room.

Allen planned on saying a lot more than two bad words by the time he got done with her. She was about to find out she was his, and he wasn't going to share her, at least not with Harold and Brad. She belonged to him, dammit.

Before he could say another word the front door opened, and Clive, his wife, Helen, Brad, Harold, and Ed walked into the foyer.

"You sons of bitches. Which one of you assholes did Lily?" Allen yelled at Brad and Harold.

Caleb was beyond mad when he realized it hadn't been his brother who had been making Lily laugh the way she had upstairs. When she had walked into the room he had been stunned. He hadn't really had time to look her over before as she had been wearing a jacket over her blouse, but now he could really see her.

She was wearing one of his old plaid shirts which she had tied at the waist, leaving her midriff peeking out. The top three buttons were undone. This allowed her ample cleavage to show. He had never realized how sexy one of his old shirts could be until then.

She was going to have to rethink if she thought they were going to stand by and let these two assholes have her. Even the thought of them touching her was more than he could handle. She was theirs, and they were willing to fight for her.

Brad and Harold looked at each other, then at Lily, who was watching Allen with horror. Clive's wife, Helen, gasped and leaned into Clive.

"I'm going to fucking kick your asses. I told you she was off-limits, but you two motherfuckers couldn't keep your pants up. Which one of you fucked her in my room?" Allen demanded, clenching his fists and taking a step toward them. All the days of watching them watch Lily came to a boil as he thought of them with their hands all over her.

Brad stuttered, "Allen. I—we—didn't touch her, I swear. You told us to leave her alone, and we did just like you said. I swear. Harold was over at the March's place helping Clem fix the roof on his barn, and I was working with the new horses in the barn all afternoon until Caleb got back. Caleb, you saw me. I took care of Buck for you, remember?" Harold just stood there dumbly, nodding his head up and down.

Ed cleared his throat, "Now, Allen. Think about what you're saying. Do you really think so little of Lily? Do you really think she would have… you know… with someone in your bedroom?"

Lily just stood there mortified. She had never been accused of something like this in all her years of working with families. She hadn't said anything at first because she just couldn't believe what Allen and Caleb were accusing her of, but the more she listened the madder she got. Straightening her shoulders, she walked over to Allen and Caleb.

"You owe me three dollars and fifty cents. I expect it to be in the nearest cursing jar by morning," Lily said, glaring up at Allen. Turning to Caleb, she glared at him too, "You owe me the same amount for even thinking what you did, plus an apology."

Lily turned and looked at Harold and Brad. "I'm sorry you were put in such an awkward situation. It was never my intention to embarrass either of you. I want you to know I enjoy your friendship and your company, and you are welcome here any time you like," Lily said stiffly.

Lily looked at Helen, Clive, and Ed. "I apologize you had to witness the lack of manners of these two men. I'm sure they will be on their best behavior for the remainder of the night, because if they aren't they will be sleeping in the barn tonight. Now, if everyone is ready for dinner, I have everything set in the dining room," she added.

Lily turned and pointed her finger at Caleb and Allen before she left the room. Glaring at them, she threatened both men in a stern voice, "If you know what's good for you, you will be on your best behavior for the rest of the night, or I swear I'll whack you both upside your heads with my broom. Do you hear me?"

Ed and Clive chuckled under their breath while Helen followed Lily out of the room with a huff. Ed said gruffly, "Boys, if I didn't know any better I'd think you were in the deep end of the manure pile tonight."

Caleb and Allen just stood in the living room, watching as everyone filed out of the room. "Well, I guess I'd better pay up, or I'll be getting cold oatmeal in the morning," Allen said quietly, pulling out his wallet and placing a five-dollar bill in the jar on the table.

"What the hell is a cursing jar, and why do I feel like the lowest life form on Earth right now?" Caleb asked, puzzled.

"Lily doesn't tolerate anyone using profanity. Anyone who does has to pay twenty-five cents per word," Allen said. "The first couple of days I was up and about was bad. I had to borrow money from Clive to pay."

"What happens if you don't pay?" Caleb asked curiously.

"You don't want to know. She comes up with all kinds of tortures. The first time she shut off the hot-water heater so I had to take cold showers, then she fed me cold, lumpy oatmeal for breakfast. The worst thing is she won't talk to you until you pay. And Caleb, she knows if you don't. I don't know how, but she knows."

Caleb looked at the jar, then back at the dining room where he could hear Lily laughing with Helen about something that was said. "Do you have five dollars I can borrow?" he asked sheepishly.

Chapter 6

The evening went well after the little incident in the living room. Lily hardly looked at Allen and Caleb, which drove both men nuts. She asked questions and listened intently as Helen talked about her and Clive's children and grandchildren. She asked Harold how Clem's roof repair went and if he was going to have to be helping out any more. She even asked Brad how the horses were doing. After dinner and dessert the two women chased the men out into the living room to talk while they cleaned up the kitchen.

"You know, both those boys feel lower than a pig's belly right now," Helen commented as she handed a dish to Lily to put up.

"They'll be all right. It serves them right thinking such horrible thoughts. Even if I had decided to be with either Harold or Brad—or both of them for that matter—it is none of their business," Lily said as she shut the door to the cabinet a little harder than necessary.

Helen smiled. "I don't think the boys feel that way. From the looks they were giving you during dinner, I'd think they wanted it to be nothing but their business."

Lily's face flushed as she looked at Helen. "Helen, I don't want the boys to think of me in that way. I'm just here temporarily."

Helen looked at Lily surprised. "But, why? You couldn't ask for any finer young men, and if Ethan feels the same way… Well, you know they've been looking for one woman to fill their life."

Lily smiled sadly at Helen. "Yes, but it's not me. When they have healed enough and no longer need help, it will be time for me to leave."

Helen started to say something, but Lily just shook her head, not wanting to discuss it further. They finished cleaning the kitchen about the time Clive came in to say it was time to go. After that everyone left. Lily looked at the clock and was surprised at how late it was. Tomorrow would come early, and there was always a lot that needed to be done.

"Lily," Allen said quietly from the doorway.

Lily looked around to see Allen and Caleb standing in the doorway watching her. Flushing a little, she licked her lips before replying. "Yes, Allen?"

Both men felt the impact of her shy tongue licking her lips. Unable to stay so far from her, they both moved, each one approaching her from a different side of the table. Lily watched uneasily as both men moved toward her. She found herself trapped between them with no escape. Allen reached her first.

Cupping her face in his hands, he murmured. "I'm sorry about earlier. I shouldn't have accused you of having sex with Harold and Brad."

Lily licked her suddenly dry lips again. "No, you shouldn't have," she whispered, turning to face him.

She felt the warmth from Caleb's body behind her, pressing her closer to Allen. Caleb slid his arms around her waist, holding her hips against the bulge in the front of his pants.

"I'm sorry, Lily. I should never have accused you of having sex in my brother's room," Caleb said softly in her ear, before adding, "At least with someone else."

Lily shivered as Caleb's warm breath fanned her neck. She arched her neck to the side, desperate to get away from the feelings washing over her. She was there for a reason, she reminded herself. She was there to help them, not be seduced by them. Not to fall in love with them. She had no room for falling in love. She had no future with them. It would only bring heartache.

Lily gasped when she felt Caleb's lips on her neck. Arching backward she unknowingly thrust her hips and breasts into Allen. Lily's eyes swung around and locked onto Allen's. She couldn't look away. Allen groaned. He had dreamed of kissing Lily every night for over a week. Every day he thought about how she would taste. He had to know. Crushing her between his body and his brother's, he captured her lips, drinking her in like a drowning man gasping for a breath.

"What the hell is going on?" a voice demanded from the doorway.

Lily broke away from Allen and groaned. "You owe me twenty-five cents. Place the money in any of the cursing jars in the house," she said huskily, unable to break her heavy gaze from looking at Allen's lips.

Allen rested his forehead on Lily's while Caleb chuckled softly. "Bad timing, bro, but welcome home."

Lily looked over to see the huge figure of Ethan Cunnings standing in the doorway. Smiling at him,

Lily asked softly, "Are you hungry? I can warm you up some roasted chicken and vegetables. Or, I have some pie left."

Ethan stood there for a moment and just watched as his brothers reluctantly let the petite female standing between them go. When he had first walked in he had thought it strange how quiet the house was. When he had left it had been filled with the sounds of crashing bottles and curses.

He had come home a few days earlier than he had planned, determined to get his family back on track. He definitely hadn't been expecting to find his two brothers enjoying a feast. He had never been so turned on in his life as when he had watched his brothers kissing the girl, at least not until she had looked at him with desire-laden eyes and asked him if he was hungry.

Oh hell yeah, he was hungry. She had the most incredible eyes. He just knew he could drown in them. He looked at her swollen lips, and his mind seemed to short-circuit. He wanted to feel her lips wrapped around him.

"I stopped on the way home," Ethan replied huskily. He only had an appetite for one thing right now, and she was standing there looking at him.

"Oh, well. In that case, I'll say goodnight to everyone," Lily said with a forced smile. "Goodnight, Ethan. Goodnight, Allen. Goodnight, Caleb. See you in the morning."

All three men stared in disbelief as Lily slipped around Caleb and closed the door to her bedroom. Running his hands through his hair, Caleb turned, leaned over, and groaned. "I don't fucking believe your timing, Ethan."

"Caleb?" a soft voice called out from behind the door.

"Yes, Lily?" Caleb groaned.

"You owe me another twenty-five cents. I heard that."

Allen started chuckling softly at first, then it grew louder until it was a full-blown belly laugh. He was laughing so hard he couldn't catch his breath. Soon, Caleb had joined him and then Ethan.

"I don't know what the hell we are laughing about, but it sure sounds good to hear you two," Ethan said.

"Ethan," Lily's husky voice called out from behind the closed door.

"I know, I know. I owe you twenty-five cents," Ethan called out. "Let's go into the living room so we don't disturb her."

"It won't matter," Allen warned. "If you cuss, she'll know, so be careful what you say. She made Brad pay up before he left here tonight for what he said to Caleb when he got home. I know she wasn't anywhere near them to hear."

Ethan walked into the living room. It was the same, but it seemed different. He couldn't quite put his finger on the change, but it just felt warmer, more like a home. Turning to look at his brothers, he was floored by the changes he saw in Allen. It had only been a little over a week since he had seen him, but it was like looking at a totally different person.

"Okay, which one of you is going to tell me who the hel— heck that was in the kitchen?" Ethan asked placing his hands on his hips.

Caleb glared at Ethan and Allen before shrugging his shoulders. "I just met her late this afternoon. All I know is her name is Lily, and I'm staking my claim on her right now."

Allen's breath hissed out sharply. "Like hel— heck you are! She's mine."

Ethan glared at both of them before asking again. "Okay. First, tell me who the hell she is?" He didn't care if he had to pay another twenty-five cents; he wanted to know who the hell she was because he was going to stake his own goddamn claim.

Allen ran his hands through his hair again before waving his brothers toward the chairs. He sat heavily on the couch and stared at the fire a moment before answering. "Her name is Lily, and she is the new housekeeper Maggie hired. She started a little over a week ago. The first time I met her, she literally knocked me on my ass." Allen grimaced and ran a hand down his face and looked at his two older brothers. "I just know since she came into my life I look forward to getting up in the morning, and I haven't needed a drink or had a nightmare. Hell, just thinking about her gives me a damn hard-on."

Both Caleb and Ethan absorbed the impact of what Allen was saying. Caleb looked at Ethan. "I just met her this afternoon, but what I felt when I just heard her was almost enough to floor me." He looked at Allen. "When I thought the two of you were getting it on in your bedroom upstairs it took everything I had in me not to join you. Probably the only thing stopping me was I needed a shave and shower. Later, when she ran into me and I held her in my arms, I knew I wasn't going to let her go."

Caleb stood up and paced back and forth in front of the fireplace before turning and shoving his hands in his front pockets. "I want her, and I don't plan on giving her up."

Ethan listened to both his brothers before replying. "I guess that makes three," he responded quietly. "I don't know why, but I know she was meant for me." Looking at his brothers again, he corrected himself. "For us. It looks like we finally found the woman we've been wishing for. Now all we have to do is convince her."

"This is the first time she's let me really touch her. We usually spend every evening in the den either talking—or I like to listen to her read to me," Allen said with a slight tinge of red seeping up his neck.

Caleb looked startled. "What was she doing in your bedroom upstairs, then? I thought for sure you and her were an item."

"I don't know. I've still been staying in the downstairs guest room."

"Well, maybe we'd better go check to see. I'd personally like to get her up in the master bedroom myself. Do any of you know her plans? Where's she from? Does she have any family?" Ethan asked as he moved toward the front staircase.

Allen shook his head. "No. It's strange. When we are together she is always asking questions about us. I never seemed to get a chance to ask her about herself."

"Well, that's about to change," Ethan replied, looking at both his brothers. "I want to know everything about her. If she turns out to be some little gold digger looking for a big haul, we'll deal with it, but I want to know."

Caleb started to say something, but Ethan shook his head as he looked at him. "It won't matter. She is ours. I just want to know her game plan so we can defuse any potential problems before they develop."

"I'm telling you, she's not like that," Allen said heatedly as he opened the door to his old bedroom. "Lily wouldn't hurt a fly."

Allen turned on the light to his old room looking around in disbelief. The covers on the bed were turned down, with colorful throw pillows arranged on it. It looked like it was ready for him to crawl into.

On his dresser was a bouquet of flowers, their scent filling the air. All his clothes were placed neatly back in his closet. A new picture of him and his brothers taken a little over a year ago stood on one nightstand. All three of them were on horseback and silhouetted by their home behind them.

Allen remembered the day well. He, Caleb, and Ethan had left early to help with the roundup. It had gone well, and they had enjoyed being together, joking and cutting up all day just like when they were boys.

Allen was shaken because the picture seemed to speak about everything that was important to him, home and family. He blinked back tears as he realized how close he had come to forgetting that over the past eight months. It humbled him to realize how much pain he had inflicted on his family because of his own anger.

Ethan laid his hand on Allen's shoulder, seeming to understand what was going through his mind. "Welcome home, Allen," he said quietly before turning and leaving the room.

Caleb just nodded to Allen before he left too. Allen stood there for several minutes trying to get his feelings under control. Gently shutting the door, he went over and sat on the edge of the bed.

For the first time since his capture and release, he cried. He cried for his lost friends and comrades. He cried for the loss of his parents. He cried for the pain he had inflicted on those he loved, but most of all he cried for the life he almost threw away out of selfishness.

Lily paused as she felt the shift in the house. It wasn't anything she could put her finger on, more like a feeling something big had just taken place. With a smile, she finished brushing out her long hair.

The brothers were reunited again. Things were going well, she thought sadly. A little too well. If the brothers once again realized how much they needed each other, then her job here would be finished. It would be time to go again.

Laying the brush down on the vanity, Lily pulled out a ragged journal, opening it up to a new page.

> *Tonight all three brothers came together and talked. Allen has come so far in the past week. I will miss our quiet evenings together. Today I fixed up*

his bedroom upstairs as a surprise for him. He is so much stronger and getting stronger every day. I love watching him work with the horses when he thinks I'm not looking. He has a gentleness to him I'm sure he would deny. I could see the love he had for Caleb.

Caleb was a surprise. I don't know why as I had studied the pictures of him hanging in Allen's room. He was so much more everything. I could see the worry in his eyes for Allen. It has been hard on him, seeing his brother in pain and not being able to do anything about it. I didn't want him to know how sweet it was of him thinking I was messing around with someone behind Allen's back. He would probably have seen the humor in it as well if he knew I had never even been kissed before. He is so protective of his younger brother.

Ethan I am not sure about as I only had a few minutes to spend with him. I could tell Ethan wanted to protect his brothers from me, unsure of my intentions. I will have to reassure him tonight will not be repeated. Ethan's whole demeanor speaks of control and authority. It will be hard to get him to let go. It seems like he has forgotten what it is like to just enjoy life. I will have to think about what I can do to help him enjoy the little things.

I received my first kiss tonight. I was so shaken I didn't know what to do. This has never happened in any of my other lives. I will need to be careful as I don't want the brothers becoming too attached to me. It will be hard enough when it is time for me to leave. My feelings are so confused. I wish I had someone to talk to.

Lily closed the journal and placed it back in her canvas bag. She turned off the light and climbed into bed. Tomorrow would be an interesting day with all three of the brothers finally home together.

Chapter 7

Peter Canton studied the wall in front of him in frustration. The wall was covered in copies of newspaper clippings along with photocopies of documents. The clippings were in chronological order starting almost a hundred years before in 1919.

Oklahoma Press

Wednesday, April 12, 1919

Mother and Daughter Killed By Local Man

The body of a local woman, Maureen O'Donnell, was found beaten and strangled to death. Her daughter, Lily O'Donnell, has not been found, but she is presumed dead. Lily O'Donnell had gone to the local sheriff complaining about threats made by James Butler, a local farmer. It is suspected Butler killed the mother before attacking the daughter and tossing her body in the local river, swollen from the recent rains. Law enforcement officials have arrested Butler after he confessed during a drunken rage. Volunteers continue to search the river for Miss O'Donnell's body. Burial for her mother will be at the Oak Grove Cemetery on April 25, in the year of our Lord 1919 at 2:00 p.m.

New York Daily News

Thursday, March 18, 1938

Local Woman Killed After Saving the Life of Wealthy Socialite

Lily O'Donnell had recently begun working as a housekeeper for wealthy New York socialite Annaise Adams, from the Adams dynasty. Mrs. Adams, the wife of hotel and merchandising baron, Andrew Adams, and mother of two had fallen ill in recent months. There has been speculation she had contracted a mysterious illness while in India last summer. Miss O'Donnell recently uncovered evidence of the poisoning of Mrs. Adams by her nephew, Albert Adams. It is suspected Albert Adams would receive a sizable insurance payoff in the event of his aunt's death. Miss O'Donnell was killed by Albert Adams during a conflict when Mr. and Mrs. Adams confronted the younger Adams with the evidence. Funeral arrangements will be announced at a later date.

The Oregon Post

Monday, September 6, 1954

Woman Stops Kidnapper From Taking Child

A man wanted on various charges entered the home of local judge Jacob Abernathy and attempted to kidnap his only son, Brandon. Local hero, Lily O'Donnell, was killed when the man opened fire with a handgun. Angus Peddles, 60, is suspected of trying to kidnap eight-year-old Brandon Abernathy in order to prevent Judge Abernathy from trying his brother, Matthew Peddles. Miss O'Donnell worked as a housekeeper for Judge Abernathy and his wife, Bernice. Miss O'Donnell is credited with notifying local authorities of the invasion by Peddles. Witnesses state that when Peddles turned a gun on Brandon and Mrs. Abernathy, Miss O'Donnell placed herself in front of it, giving authorities time to rescue them. Efforts to save her were unsuccessful. Funeral arrangements are pending.

Louisiana Post

May 27, 1978

Local Woman Saves Man From Drowning

Michael Evans, a local widower, was saved from drowning by a local woman after his car ran off the road during heavy rains. The woman, Lily O'Donnell, was pronounced dead at the scene. Ms. O'Donnell worked as a housekeeper for Angelina Brunson, New Orleans socialite and owner of The Shrimp Pot. Funeral arrangements are pending for Ms. O'Donnell.

Louisiana Post

August 30, 1980

Marriage Announcements: Michael Evans and Angelina Brunson have announced their engagement.

Peter looked at the last clipping. It was over thirty years old, but showed the same young woman in it as the other articles. He studied the picture of Lily O'Donnell taken in 1917 with her parents. It was grainy, but it was unmistakably the same young woman, unchanged except for her clothing.

Peter had first come across her in the 1978 story. He had been working in New Orleans at The Shrimp Pot. He had seen pictures of Lily O'Donnell with both Michael Evans' children and with Angelina Brunson. When he had inquired about it, a strange, twisted tale came out about how Lily had been a big help to Michael Evans during his wife's illness and subsequent death two years before. She had discovered Evans' first love had been Angelina before she had married a man named Brunson. She had maintained contact with the family while she worked with Angelina Brunson, a widow herself. While in the hospital, Brunson had visited Evans and discovered he was her childhood sweetheart. If it had not been for Lily's death, they would never have met again.

It wasn't until Peter was serving an older man who had come on vacation with his wife that he had begun doing his research. The man had insisted the picture of Lily hanging on the wall with Angelina Brunson was the same Lily O'Donnell, who had saved him when he was a boy.

Everyone had thought he was senile until the man had pulled a folded newspaper article out of his wallet and showed it Peter. Peter went home that night and did a search for Lily's name on the Internet.

He had been surprised at what he had found. At first he couldn't believe it. As he printed out the pictures and did more and more research he noticed a pattern. In each case Lily's body disappeared before it was buried. In the first case her body had never been found. In each case afterward her body had disappeared from the morgue as soon as it arrived. No one had any explanations as to what had happened, just that her body must have been misplaced.

The only thing Peter wanted to know was when and where Lily was going to appear next. He wanted to find her. At forty-seven, he didn't want to get any older. It appeared Lily had discovered the fountain of youth, and he wanted a drink of it. To do that, he needed to find her before she disappeared again. He had set up his computer to do daily searches for her. He had been doing this for the past ten years with no luck. Looking at the photos, though, he felt sure that his luck was about to change.

Chapter 8

Helen came over the next morning with Clive. She and Lily had made arrangements to attend a local women's group festival. The Boulder Flats Women's Club raised money each year to help local families buy food and Christmas gifts. Helen was the treasurer and had talked Lily into coming to help deliver food boxes to the local merchants.

The newspaper was going to be doing an article to help advertise the event. Helen had said having a pretty girl in the picture would help get the men's attention. Lily had just shaken her head and laughed at Helen's nonsense. Allen, Ethan, and Caleb had all growled and groaned.

Ethan had decided he was going to do a personal interview with Lily to learn more about her. Caleb and Allen had decided they would take her horseback riding if the weather was good. Now, all their well laid plans lay in shambles around their feet.

Caleb frowned when he saw Lily come out of the kitchen wearing her thin patchwork jacket. "Where do you think you are going?" he asked sternly.

"With Helen. She's warming her car up now," Lily said as she zipped up the front of her jacket and pulled her long braid out from under it.

"Where's your jacket? The one you are wearing isn't appropriate for the weather outside," Caleb asked impatiently.

"I don't have one yet. I'm waiting until I've earned enough from the cursing jars to buy one," Lily replied, walking to the front door. "At the rate you guys are filling them up, it shouldn't be much longer," Lily added with a cheeky grin.

"Very funny. What do you mean you don't have one? Are you telling me you've been going out to the barn and collecting eggs for the past week wearing this thing?" Caleb growled, pushing Lily gently back against the door and placing his hands on either side of her, caging her in.

"What's going on?" Ethan asked as he walked into the living room from the office down the hall. Allen was close behind him.

Caleb didn't even turn around. He held Lily's shoulders as he glared down at her. "She doesn't have a decent damn jacket and thinks I'm going to let her out of the house in the one she's wearing."

Lily sighed. "Caleb. You really don't need to use profanity to describe my jacket. There is nothing wrong with it."

"Like hell there isn't," Allen said hotly.

Ethan folded his huge arms across his chest and looked sternly at Lily. "My brothers are right. You need a decent coat if you are going to live here."

Lily rolled her eyes at the three men at the same time a horn honked out front. "I'm going to be in a warm car, then a warm building. I'll pick up a coat later." Leaning up she went to brush a kiss along Caleb's cheek, only he turned his head at the last minute, sealing his lips to hers. Lily's lips parted in a startled gasp, and Caleb took advantage of it, slipping his tongue into her mouth.

Groaning, Caleb had known it was going to be sweet kissing Lily, but he had not expected it to be this sweet. Letting his hands slide down her arms, he grasped her wrists and pulled them up above her head. He wanted to stretch her out and plant his hard body in hers. Feeling a shiver run through her, he pressed his body up against hers, pinning her against the front door. Groans from the other two men filled the air as they watched Caleb kissing the woman they all wanted.

Gasping for a breath, Lily opened her eyes to stare into Caleb's dark brown ones. "I have to go," she said desperately.

"Never," Caleb replied. "I'll never let you go, Lily."

Ethan and Allen came over to stand on each side of them. With her arms still held high above her head Lily shuddered when she felt Allen's and Ethan's hands running over her face and neck. "Please, I can't do this. You shouldn't be doing this."

"Why not, Lily?" Ethan asked softly. "Tell us why we shouldn't do this?"

Lily turned eyes suddenly shining with unshed tears toward Ethan. "Because I won't be here long."

Before any of the men could ask her what she meant a knock sounded on the front door, followed by the rattling of the door knob. Lily heaved a shuddering sigh of relief as she broke Caleb's hold on her wrists and hurriedly opened the door.

Helen was standing outside looking at the brothers with a raised eyebrow. "You ready, Lily?"

"Yes," Lily said quietly. "I'll be back later."

Ethan grabbed her hand as she walked out the door, making her pause. "Later, Lily. We'll talk later." Lily shook her head back and forth.

"Helen, stop and help Lily find a decent coat. Tell Pete to put it on our tab. Get her whatever she needs, whether she thinks she needs it or not," Ethan ordered.

Lily flashed her eyes angrily at the three men standing in the doorway. "I'll get what I need with my own money." With that she stomped down the steps and slid into the waiting car.

Helen looked at the boys, then back at Lily. "I'll see what I can do, Ethan. She's just as stubborn as the three of you put together, I imagine. Don't worry. I'll take care of her and have her home before dark tonight. There are plenty of leftovers for you to warm up."

Ethan, Allen, and Caleb watched as Helen drove off. Allen slammed his fist into the door frame. "Dammit! Do you fucking know how hard I am just watching you kiss her?" Allen turned and strode down the hall into the office.

Ethan and Caleb looked at each other. They were suffering too. They followed Allen into the office and sat down. Stretching his long legs out in front of him, Caleb looked squarely at his brothers. "What the fuck did she mean by she wouldn't be here long?"

Allen was standing in front of the window looking down the long drive. He was shaking. He looked at his hands and saw they were trembling. "I can't even think about her leaving. It tears me up inside." He glanced at his brothers before turning to look back outside.

Ethan said quietly, "Then we won't let her go. I don't care if we have to tie her up until she realizes she belongs here with us. None of us has ever felt this way before. When the dads told us what it was like when they first saw Mom, I thought they were full of shit. Now I know they weren't. Shit, I haven't even kissed her or held her yet, and I'm freaking fixing to blow. Watching you two with her had me hotter than a Fourth of July barbecue last night."

* * *

Lily drew in a deep breath. She was glad the car was warm because she was shaking like a leaf. She had to figure out a way to keep the men at a distance. Clasping her hands together tightly in her lap, she closed her eyes, trying to calm her racing pulse.

The feel of all three of the brothers' hands on her had been overwhelming. She had almost self-combusted from the rush of fire that raced through her. She was so confused. She wasn't supposed to get so attached to those she came to help.

Each of the families she had been with had loved her but never where it would be so devastating that they couldn't function if she was no longer in their lives. She had made sure of that. With each family she had helped she had made sure she'd maintained a respectful distance emotionally. How could this have happened? She didn't try to encourage them. In fact, she had tried very hard to maintain a distance, ensuring they would just be friends.

During the week she and Allen had spent together, she had made sure she kept him busy from morning to dusk. At first she had hidden in the den at night until he had discovered her hiding place. Then she had made sure she sat in a single chair, forcing him to sit either on the small couch or the other chair. She had asked lots of questions about his family. She wanted him to remember all the good things.

Lily was so lost in thought she jerked when Helen spoke. "Do you want to talk about it?"

Lily looked through the window of the car at the passing landscape before she finally spoke. "I'm so confused. I don't know what they want from me. I'm afraid it is more than I can give them."

Helen glanced sideways briefly before refocusing on the road ahead of her. "They want you, Lily. They want you to be a part of their lives. All of them. Do you have a problem with that?"

Helen listened carefully to Lily's response. She and Clive had talked about it last night after they had left. It was obvious how much Lily had affected the two younger Cunnings men.

After seeing how Ethan reacted to her, Helen had no doubt he felt the same. It took a strong woman to handle three big Wyoming men. It took a special woman. Helen felt confident Lily was just such a woman, but sometimes other things factor into a woman's decision. Most people had a problem with one woman being with three men. In Boulder Flats it wouldn't be a problem. There were a number of couples living in or around the area who were happily married to more than one man or woman.

"It's not that," Lily started to say.

"Then what is it?" Helen asked gently, not wanting to push Lily into saying something she wasn't ready to admit.

Lily looked out the window again trying to hold back the tears. "Helen, I can't let them get close to me. Not in a way that will affect them long term. I need them to find the strength they had as a family, then find a woman to share it with. Another woman, not me."

"Why not you, Lily? Do you think you aren't good enough for them? Is there someone else? Why can't you be the woman they need? The woman they love and want to spend the rest of their lives with?"

"Because I won't be here very long. I can't explain to you why, so please don't ask." Lily clenched her hands together even tighter. "Helen, if anything should ever happen to me will you do me a favor?"

Helen's breath caught in her throat. It sounded like Lily already knew something would happen. But how could she? "Of course, honey."

"In my room there is a canvas bag. In the bag is a journal. It won't be there for long, so you will have to hurry. I'd like for you to give it to Allen, Ethan, and Caleb. I can't explain what I'm telling you, but you must promise me you'll give it to them if you can," Lily finished in a rush.

She had never wanted anyone to know about her. About her life. But now it seemed important for the men to know who she really was, and if she had had a choice she would have made the choice to stay with them.

Puzzled, Helen agreed. Lily quickly turned the conversation to what the ladies did and what they were going to be doing. The rest of the day flew by. The local newspaper reporter came by and interviewed all the ladies before taking a picture for the front page. Lily had a wonderful time laughing and joking with the women. Helen insisted they go by Pete's Trade Stop to pick up the items Lily needed, stating she didn't want Clive to have to get in trouble for her not following the bosses' orders.

Lily had grudgingly conceded, picking out only the bare necessities and getting a total so she could subtract it from her first paycheck. There was more than one way to win a battle. On the ride home Helen told Lily about how their children and grandchildren were flying in for a big Christmas. Lily laughed at the antics of some of the grandkids. In all too short a time, Helen was pulling up in front of the ranch house.

"Thanks for inviting me, Helen. I had a wonderful time," Lily said as she climbed out of the car and gathered her packages together.

"I'll come by in a couple days, and we can plan Thanksgiving dinner. We used to do a big spread for all the men who stayed on over the holiday," Helen said.

"Sounds great. Bye." Lily waved before turning and walking up the steps. The front door opened before she had even reached the top step. All three of the brothers stood in the doorway. Lily stopped for a minute and just stared at them.

"Is this all you bought?" Allen said with disapproval.

"Yes. It's all I need. I believe that was your stipulation," Lily said with a frustrated grunt.

Caleb frowned at Lily. "I think we should have taken you to town. You need more than what those measly bags can hold."

"Let me see what you bought," Ethan said, reaching for a bag.

Before Lily could stop them, Ethan and Caleb had taken the bags out of her hands, and Allen had pulled her close against his body. Ushering her into the living room, Ethan and Caleb began pulling items out.

"What are you doing?" Lily demanded. "You can't go through those. They are mine."

Ethan growled at Lily when she tried to pull a smaller bag out of his hands. "Who paid for it?"

Lily flushed. "I put it on your account because Helen wouldn't let me do anything else, but I have the receipt and I plan on paying you back when I get my first paycheck. Now give me my things, or I swear I'll take them all back," Lily retorted hotly.

"Not until we see what you bought. You needed more than a jacket. Do you think we haven't noticed you were wearing some of our old shirts out of the rag pile Maggie kept down in the basement?" Allen said, wrapping his arms around Lily's waist and pulling her snugly against his hard frame.

Lily blushed even redder. "There is nothing wrong with them, and they are comfortable. It wasn't like you guys would miss them."

"You're damn right about that," Caleb said, pulling a sweater and a long-sleeved shirt out of one bag. "How could I miss you wearing my shirt all tied up at the waist, showing off your delectable belly button."

Lily wiggled against Allen. He tightened his arms around her, sliding his hand up to rest under her breast.

Ethan whistled as he opened the smaller bag. Grinning, he pulled out several pairs of lacy underwear. "I had no idea Pete sold this stuff."

Lily closed her eyes, groaning in embarrassment.

"Aw hell, Lily. I know I've never seen those in Pete's store," Allen said huskily.

Lily twisted in his arms and glared up at him. "How would you know, Allen? Do you often look for women's lingerie?" she asked with a raised eyebrow.

Allen stared intently down at Lily. "I do now."

Lily shivered. Before she could twist back around, Allen crushed her lips to his. He kissed her deeply. It was only when she felt another warm body behind her that Allen released her mouth. He turned her slowly around until her back was pressed against his front. When Lily looked up, she was staring into Ethan's intense eyes.

"My turn. Do you have any idea how hard it is to watch my brothers touch you and kiss you when I haven't had a chance to do it yet?" Ethan whispered. "It's my turn now."

Without any other warning Ethan's hard arms came around Lily, pulling her up against him until she had to raise her legs and wrap them around his waist. Ethan sucked in a breath before he crushed his own lips down onto Lily's. Nipping at her lips to open, he drank deeply, not giving Lily a chance to protest or retreat.

Lily vaguely heard groaning in the background and wasn't sure if it came from her or from the two other men in the room. Her stomach clenched, and farther down she felt something she had never felt before. She kissed Ethan back with all the hunger of someone starved for love. Running her hands through his hair, she tugged him, pulling his head further down, trying to get even closer to him.

"Damn, but she is on fire," Caleb croaked out hoarsely. He moved up to one side of Lily, rubbing his hands over her ass and up her back. Lily moaned and arched backward, thrusting her hips down onto Ethan's hard length.

"Shit," Ethan said in a strangled voice. "The guest bedroom. I'll never make it to the master bedroom."

Lily vaguely heard them through a fog of longing and need. She shouldn't be doing this. It would complicate things when she left. She didn't want to hurt them, but she was so tired of always being alone. She burned for them.

She felt the soft covers of the bed as Ethan laid her gently down on it. She felt hands slowly unbuttoning her blouse and pulling it out of her jeans. She felt them as they unbuttoned the top buttons on her jeans. All she could do was feel as their hands moved over her flat stomach and full breasts. A set of lips grabbed her swollen nipple through the lace of her bra. Lily cried out, almost lifting straight off the bed.

"I love you, Lily," Allen said softly in her ear, running little kisses down her face and along her jawline.

Lily froze. No, she couldn't do this. She knew what it was like to love and lose someone. She knew the horrendous pain one felt at seeing a love one who had died. She couldn't, wouldn't do that to anyone. Especially, not these men who had known so much pain.

Pushing against their hands, Lily cried out. "Stop. Stop. Please stop."

Struggling to sit up, she backed away, not wanting to look at the three men who had come to mean so much to her in such a short time. Pulling her shirt together, she tried to button it with shaking hands.

Ethan reached for her, but stopped when she shook her head. "Lily, what's wrong? You know we wouldn't hurt you."

Crying, Lily pulled her knees up to her chest and wrapped her arms around her legs. "I told you, I can't do this. I can't be with you."

"You're ours, Lily. You fucking know it too. You want us just as much as we want you," Caleb said frustrated.

Allen placed his hand on Caleb's arm trying to get him to calm down. "Is it because I told you I love you, Lily? Is that why you're scared?" Allen asked quietly. "Because if it is, it won't change a thing. I'll still love you. I can't speak for my brothers, but I've spent enough time with you to know I want you to be a part of my life. I want to spend the rest of my life with you. I miss our evenings together. I ache for you every damn day and night."

Lily scooted across the bed and stood up straight. She took a deep breath before looking up at the three men staring at her. Shaking her head back and forth, she begged them softly.

"Please, don't love me. You don't understand. You shouldn't love me. You aren't supposed to fall in love with me. I won't be here for long. Please understand. It's not you. It's me. You need to find someone else. Someone who will be here for you, someone who can love you the way I can't," she whispered.

"What do you mean when you say you won't be here for long, Lily?" Ethan asked softly. "You've said that before. Why? Why can't you stay here? Why can't we love you?"

Lily just stood there staring at the three of them with tears pouring down her face. She couldn't answer them. What could she say? She wasn't really alive. She didn't know what she was, but she never stayed long when she came to help someone.

"Fuck this. When you decide you want to stay, you let us know," Caleb growled in a deep voice. He turned and walked out of the room. A minute later they all heard the front door slam.

Ethan walked over to Lily and looked down at her bent head. "When you are ready to talk, we'll be here for you. We're going to love you whether you want us to or not. You already mean more than you can imagine to all of us." He quietly walked out of the room.

Allen just stood staring at Lily for a moment before gently giving the top of her head a soft kiss and walking out the door as well. She broke down when she heard the door open and close.

Holding her blouse together, she slowly walked into the living room and gathered up the few purchases she had made. She walked through the darkened kitchen and into her room, shutting and locking the door.

The kitten glanced up as she turned on the light beside her bed. It stretched and yawned really big before running its little body around Lily's legs. She smiled through her tears. Bending down, she picked up the little fuzzy body and held it close to her heart.

"I don't know how, but somehow I'll figure out what I am supposed to do now," she murmured. "You wouldn't have any suggestions would you?" The kitten looked up and purred contently. "I didn't think so."

* * *

The next morning the men were quiet during breakfast. The silence was killing Lily. This was not what was supposed to be happening. Allen watched her intently, but never said a word. Caleb was withdrawn, barely eating anything before he slammed his hat on and said he had work to do. Ethan finished his meal, picked up his coffee cup, and disappeared in the direction of the office. Allen got up a few minutes later and walked over to where Lily was wiping down the countertop. He ran his hand down over her hair before pulling his hat on and walking out the door.

The next week was the same thing. Meals were a tense affair. If anything, Lily felt more lost and lonely than ever before. Unable to stand it any longer, she called Helen and asked if she could come pick her up. Lily had to talk to someone, and Helen was the only one she felt she could confide in.

Caleb looked up from where he was talking with Ed and Brad when he saw the car pull up. He watched as Lily came down the steps of the house and got into the car. Clive walked up behind him as he watched his wife pull away.

"Do you know where Helen's taking Lily?" Caleb asked as he watched the car moving down the long drive.

Clive spat before answering. "Helen just said they needed some girl time together. She has taken a fancy to Lily."

Caleb looked toward the house and saw Ethan and Allen standing in different parts of the house watching Helen drive away with Lily. They felt it too. A fear they couldn't quite put their fingers on.

Turning back to the matter at hand, Caleb gave both his brothers a nod. It was hard on them, but they had talked and decided they needed to give Lily time to make up her mind what she wanted. As far as they were concerned there was no doubt. They wanted her. Forever. If she needed time to come to terms with it, they were willing to wait.

Each of the men was handling it in their own way. Ethan buried himself in his work. Caleb bottled everything up and tried to ignore it, but Allen was the one having the hardest time. He never said anything to Lily, but he had to touch her. It was tearing him apart in a totally different way than what he had gone through during his capture. It was like a little piece of him was missing.

Helen drove for a few miles before she spoke. "Do you want to talk about it?"

Lily pushed her hair away from her face and peeked at Helen. "They hardly talk to me anymore," Lily began.

"Do you mind me asking what happened?" Helen probed gently.

Lily sighed, looking out the window of the car before replying softly. "Allen told me he loved me. I didn't handle it very well."

Helen smiled. "All three of those boys adore you."

Lily turned and looked at Helen. "What am I going to do? It will break their hearts when I'm gone. How can I love them knowing I won't be with them for long?"

Helen glanced at Lily before looking back at the road thoughtfully. "Are you so sure you won't be staying this time?"

"Yes," came the soft reply.

"It's said it is better to have loved and lost than to have never loved at all. Maybe you need to just let yourself love those boys with all your heart for as long as you've got. That is all you can do. That is all any of us can do. There are never any guarantees on how long we'll be on this earth," Helen said.

Lily thought about what Helen said for a while. Could she do that? Could she love them with everything in her knowing it wouldn't be for long? Could she overcome her fear of losing them? Wasn't that what she was really afraid of?—her own heart breaking when the time came for her to say good-bye.

Taking a deep breath, she felt the tension slowly melt out of her as she came to accept her decision. Helen was right. She might not have very long with the men she loved, but she had a short time. She would just have to make sure she loved them enough to last a lifetime.

"Thank you, Helen. I guess I was just too afraid to make the decision to grab what I wanted before it was too late," Lily smiled shyly.

Helen smiled, reaching over to pat Lily's hand. "You're welcome, dear. I promise you won't regret it."

Lily laughed, feeling more light-hearted than ever. "Let's go get the stuff for Thanksgiving dinner. I want it to be the best one the guys have ever had."

Helen parked in front of the grocery store. "Sounds like a plan."

* * *

The two women laughed as they planned a special Thanksgiving dinner, unaware they were being watched. Peter Canton sat in the diner across the street sipping coffee, a local newspaper article lying on the table in front of him. He had been in town for the past three days trying to find the woman in the photo on the front page.

He figured she would have to buy groceries sooner or later. The diner had been the perfect place to sit and watch. It was warm and had a front-row seat to anyone coming or going from the grocery store.

He had to make up a story to get the woman and two men working at the diner off his case. He had told them his car had broken down, and he was waiting for parts and money to be sent from his sister in California. They had finally left him alone after the first day.

Now he studied the car and the woman who was with Lily. He looked at the picture and identified her as Helen Simmons. She was expendable as far as Peter was concerned. He just wanted Lily.

He casually threw some money down on the table and walked out. He needed to get to his car. He had hidden it down the street out of view of the diner. He pulled the collar up on his coat to protect his neck from the icy wind. Soon, it wouldn't matter. Once he was immortal, he wouldn't care how cold it got.

Sliding into the car, he turned on the heater to full blast until the car warmed up. Sitting, he waited patiently for the two women to leave. He needed to follow them so he could learn where Lily was staying. Once he knew, he could plan on how he was going to kidnap her and force her to share all her little secrets with him.

He rubbed his hands together to warm them. He hadn't realized from the photos just how beautiful she really was. He might have to have a little fun with her first.

* * *

Lily and Helen were laughing as they hauled in the last of the grocery bags. Helen stayed long enough to help Lily put everything up before giving her a kiss and a whispered word of encouragement. Lily put on a casserole to cook slowly while she went into her room to shower and change.

She had made up her mind she was going to grab life with both hands and hold on to it as long as she was given. Wasn't this what she was supposed to help Ethan with after all? How could she help any of them if she was too afraid to do it herself? Caleb wasn't the only one bottling up his emotions.

Lily realized she had been doing that her whole life. Now she was going to show the men just how much they meant to her. She was going to love them with every fiber in her being and accept whatever they gave her back. For the first time in her whole existence she felt free.

She took a shower, enjoying the hot water as it caressed her skin. Next, she used a lightly scented lotion Helen had bought her before slipping on a form-fitting sweater dress in a dark red that emphasized her large breasts and narrow waist. Helen had taken her to a little shop in town and told her the dress and heels were her Christmas presents, ignoring Lily's protests.

Helen had also talked to Clive, and Ed and the other guys who were going over to their house for dinner. Tonight it would just be Lily, Ethan, Allen, and Caleb. She left her hair down. She had never left it down or unbraided before as it was so long. It went past her narrow waist, falling in soft waves around her rounded ass.

She felt very feminine and sexy, something she hadn't thought she would ever feel. She could feel the moisture gathering between her legs and hoped it was a good sign. She was very nervous. What if they didn't want her anymore? What would they expect? She didn't have a clue as to what she was doing.

Rubbing her hands down her thighs, she patted the little kitten who had watched her as she had gotten ready. "Wish me luck tonight," she whispered as she walked into the kitchen.

Lily glanced nervously at the clock for the fifth time. What if they didn't come home tonight? They had never missed dinner with her before, but what if they had gotten tired of waiting and found someone else to fill their needs?

Lily was on the verge of a panic attack by the time she heard the front door open and the voices of the three men as they came in. Turning around, she grabbed the pot holders and bent over to pull the casserole out of the oven.

Allen was the first one through the door. When he saw the tight red dress glued to Lily's rounded ass he froze. Caleb and Ethan had been talking quietly and didn't see Allen until it was too late.

Running into Allen's back, Caleb grunted. "What's your problem?"

Allen didn't say a word, his eyes glued to the long bare legs and round ass that were more than his vocal cords could handle.

Lily straightened and turned, holding the hot casserole in between the oven mitts. She carefully set the casserole on the table, and bending over she set out the silverware. Smiling up at the men, she didn't realize just how appetizing she looked. The sweater dress had a scooped neck showing off a large amount of cleavage. If that wasn't enough, the dress fit Lily like a second skin, showcasing her dark hair and deep blue eyes. Lily nervously pushed her hair out of the way.

Allen walked into the kitchen, making a beeline around the table and going straight to Lily. He gently reached out and touched her hair, running his fingers through the long lengths.

Lily nervously bit her lip. "I don't wear it down very often because it is so long. I've thought of cutting it off, but have never had the nerve to."

"It's beautiful," Allen replied in a deep voice, sending shivers racing down Lily's spine. "Just like you, Lily."

Lily raised her hand and placed it gently against Allen's cheek. Running her fingers along his straight nose and touching his lips, she said softly, "I was so afraid."

She looked into Allen's eyes before looking over at Caleb and Ethan who were standing still right inside the door to the kitchen. "But I'm not any more. I want to spend what time I have with you. Loving you. Will you accept that? Can you? I can't give you any guarantees except I will love all three of you with all my heart for as long as I can." Lily looked straight into Caleb's eyes as she said the last part, wanting him to know she was opening her heart and soul for him.

Caleb walked slowly toward Lily. Lily watched him fearfully. Would he accept what she was offering? Would he demand something she couldn't give him?

Caleb looked down into Lily's eyes. His heart stuttered for a moment as he heard what Lily was saying. She was opening herself up to them, offering her love and herself unconditionally. He, better than anyone, knew there were no guarantees in life. If she was offering everything she could to them he could do no less.

Wrapping his arms around her, he drew her into his arms and kissed her gently on the lips. "I love you, Lily."

"I love you, too." Lily looked at all three men. "I love you all. I want to be with you and live life like I have never been able to before. I want to share your life and your love," she whispered.

Ethan cleared his throat. "I don't know about my brothers, but the only thing I'm hungry for is you."

Lily laughed and moved into Ethan's arms. "I'm hungry for you too." Looking mischievously over her shoulder, she gave the other two a sexy smile. "For all of you."

"Shit." Caleb strode over and before anyone could say anything he swung Lily up in his arms and headed for the stairs. "Master bedroom."

Lily laughed as Caleb took the stairs two at a time. Ethan hurried ahead to open the door while Allen started stripping off his shirt. "We all need to get a shower before we come to you," Allen said as he headed for the shower in the master bathroom. "Ethan and Caleb will help you undress, then I'll take over while they get a shower. We plan on taking all night."

Lily shivered at the promise in Allen's voice. Caleb gently set Lily down in front of him and slowly ran his hands down her sides. Lily could feel the moisture pool between her legs.

Ethan moved behind her and lifted her long hair out of the way so he could slip the zipper down. Caleb stepped back so he could watch as Ethan slowly pulled the dress down Lily's body. His breath caught in his throat and his cock jerked as her breasts came free of the dress, leaving them covered by just a thin red lace bra.

"Damn, Lily. You are so fucking beautiful," Caleb choked out. Lily shivered as Ethan continued pulling the dress down until it lay at her feet. She stepped out of the dress, moving to take off her matching red high heels. "No, leave them on." Caleb began unbuttoning his shirt. "Turn around. I want to see you from behind, and I want Ethan to get a look at the view I had. I want to watch him to see how fucking hard he gets when he sees you."

Lily laughed nervously as she turned around giving Caleb a view of her back and ass. "You know you are going to owe me a pile of quarters by the time we get done."

"I'll give you the whole fucking ranch worth of quarters, darling," Caleb replied huskily as he viewed the curve of her back down along her ass. She was wearing a pair of matching red lacy panties that barely covered her sweet ass. He groaned as he thought of what it would look like to have his cock buried there.

Allen came out of the bathroom with nothing but a towel wrapped around his waist. "Fuck!" he said hoarsely. "Go get your goddamn showers and make it quick. I don't know if I have the willpower to resist her."

"You better fucking wait. This first time I want all of us to be with her," Ethan said with a growl. "I'm going to my room. I don't want to wait for you, Caleb."

Ethan headed out the door while Caleb started for the bathroom. Caleb paused before he entered the bathroom and turned to look at Lily. "I want you to stay where you are. I don't want you to move until I get back. And Lily, leave your damn shoes on. When I fuck you, I want you wearing them." Caleb turned and was stripped out of his clothes before he made it all the way into the bathroom.

Allen watched as Lily turned toward him. He cleared his throat. "You heard him. Stand still. I want to look at you." He watched as Lily shifted nervously. She glanced over her shoulder once as Allen walked around her. He watched her intently. "Don't move," he said, slapping her gently on the ass.

He pulled the towel away from his straining body. Lily's eyes widened when she saw how big and long he was. Her eyes jerked up to look into Allen's dark eyes.

"Spread your legs apart," Allen said as he ran his hands up Lily's legs, pulling them a little further apart. He continued his journey, pausing at the top of her thighs just shy of her moist mound.

Lily couldn't suppress the groan from escaping from her. She arched toward Allen's hands searching for something, desperate to find it.

"What do you want, Lily?" Allen asked softly.

Sobbing, Lily moved restlessly. "You. Touch me, Allen. Please, I ache."

Running his finger along the top of her silky red panties, Allen leaned over and whispered against her ear. "Where do you want me to touch you, Lily? Tell me."

"Anywhere, everywhere. Please. I don't know. I'm burning," Lily begged.

Ethan and Caleb came into the room, stopping as they heard Lily begging Allen to touch her. "Fuck," Ethan said. "I don't know how long I'm gonna last. She is so fucking beautiful."

Caleb stared intently at Lily. He moved with the grace of a lion tracking its prey. "Lily," he said quietly waiting for her eyes to meet his.

Licking her lips, Lily looked into Caleb's eyes. "Yes?"

"Who do you belong to?" Caleb asked quietly, walking slowly around her trembling form.

"You, Caleb. You and Allen and Ethan. I belong to all of you," Lily said with a soft tremble. She was shaking so hard she was amazed she hadn't fallen into a puddle on the floor.

"Ethan, take her bra off her. Allen, slide her panties down her legs, nice and slow. I want to watch her as you finish undressing her for the first time." Lily shivered as Ethan moved behind her and slowly undid her bra, running his hands over her back as he did it.

"Each of us will tell the other what to do at one time or another. Caleb drew the short straw, so tonight is his, but it won't always be him. Sometimes I'll lead, other times Allen," Ethan murmured in Lily's ear softly. "There will be times when we have you alone, but you will always belong to all of us. Never forget that, Lily. You are ours just like we are yours."

Lily's head tilted backward as Ethan slowly slid her bra straps down her arms and let it drop on the floor. He ran small kisses up and down her neck while he talked to her. Lily stiffened as Allen began pulling her panties down. She had never felt so vulnerable or so free in all her lives. Allen sank down to his knees as he pulled the panties slowly down her hips to pool around her ankles.

Caleb held himself still. "Lily, step out of your panties, then spread your legs wider apart. I want to watch as Allen laps your cream. Ethan, play with those beautiful breasts. I want to see how hard and big you can make her nipples." Lily cried out when she felt Allen's hot breath on her mound. She would have fallen if Ethan hadn't had his arms wrapped around her playing with her nipples.

Lily cried out again as Ethan squeezed her nipples hard. "Damn, she likes that, Ethan. Do it again," Allen muttered.

Lily began shaking uncontrollably. "Please," she gasped.

"Please what, Lily? What do you want?" Caleb asked, running his hand down her cheek. "Tell me what you want."

"I don't know. I burn so deep. Please. Help me. I want you so bad." Lily cried out again as another wave of desire raced through her to her pussy, making her ache with an incredible need.

"This is how you make us feel inside, Lily. This is how we've been burning for you since the first time we saw you. I've burned every fucking night wanting to bury myself inside your pussy," Caleb said as he gripped Lily's long hair in one of his hands. "You are ours, Lily. You are never going to leave us, do you understand. If you try, we'll fucking find you and bring you back. You belong here, Lily. You belong here with us." Caleb kissed Lily savagely. All his fear of losing her, all his love for her overwhelming him to the point he had to show her how he felt. It was too much to keep bottled up inside any longer. He needed her like the very breath he breathed.

Pulling away from her, he gasped. "Put her on the bed. Hold her arms down, Ethan. I can't wait any longer," Caleb demanded hoarsely. He watched as Allen stood suddenly, catching Lily as her knees gave way. Ethan ripped the bedspread down off the bed and helped Allen as he gently laid Lily down on the edge of the bed.

Ethan took up a position on one side of the bed, pulling Lily's right arm up and sucking on her right breast as Allen moved next to her left side, holding her arm over her head and sucking on her left breast. Lily sobbed, wanting to feel Caleb deep inside her. Caleb pulled Lily's legs up until her knees hooked over his arms. Positioning himself between her legs, he waited a moment.

"Look at me, Lily." He paused until she looked deep into his eyes. "I love you."

"I love you too, Caleb," Lily whispered as she let her love shine from her eyes.

Caleb stared deeply into Lily's eyes as he thrust forward, breaking through the thin barrier and claiming her. Lily gasped as Caleb took her, but never looked away from his eyes, wanting him to see how much she loved him.

"Shit, you are so tight, Lily," Caleb whispered hoarsely.

Sweat beaded on Caleb's forehead as he tried to give Lily time to adjust to his size. It was too much, though, as he watched his brothers sucking on her breasts and listening to her mews of delight. Pulling almost all the way out, he thrust in again. She was so slick. He pulled almost all the way out again, gripping her legs even tighter, before he pushed back in again even farther.

It was too much. He could feel his body starting to shake. He wasn't going to last long. He wanted to make sure she came before he did, but he wasn't sure he was going to make it.

Suddenly Lily jerked, arching into the mouths sucking on her breasts, and cried out. Caleb's yell followed as he thrust in once more, holding himself as still as his shaking body would let him, emptying himself deep into Lily's womb.

"Fuck it all to hell, she's clamping down on me. Oh, baby, you feel so good." Caleb leaned forward as his brothers moved, brushing Lily's hair away from her face as she cried out over and over.

She was twisting and turning so much she was driving Caleb even further into her. "God, baby. You're killing me." Caleb slowly pulled away, reaching for the towel he had dropped on the floor. Cleaning himself, he moved to lie next to Lily, running his hand up and down her body.

"Turn her over. Lily, do you think you can handle me, baby?" Allen asked hoarsely.

"Allen, I'm on fire. I want you. What's happening to me?" Lily asked desperately. "I feel like I'm going to explode."

Her whole body was one big sensitive nerve. Caleb's possession of her combined with the other two men sucking on her breasts was more than she could take. Her body seemed to explode, but she wanted more. She needed more. She felt like her body was just coming alive, and the burning deep inside her craved more.

"Caleb, help her get on her hands and knees. Ethan, take her mouth. I want to watch her beautiful lips wrapped around you while I fuck her from behind," Allen said as he wrapped his arms around Lily, grabbing her large breasts in his hands. "Damn, her tits are so big they overflow in my hands." Sliding his cock into her slick pussy, Allen groaned as he buried himself all the way to his balls. "Fuck, she is tight. You feel so good, baby."

"Allen," Lily groaned as she felt the fullness of Allen sliding into her wet pussy.

He felt bigger, wider than Caleb. He seemed to stretch her even further, to the point it was almost painful. She moaned when she felt him beginning to move. Unable to stop herself, she leaned back into Allen when he pulled almost all the way out. She let out a startled cry when she felt his hand leave her breast long enough to give her a stinging slap on her ass.

"Open your mouth, Lily. I want to watch you swallow Ethan," Allen said harshly.

Both Ethan and Caleb groaned as Lily opened her mouth to slowly take Ethan's huge cock into her mouth. He was bigger than either Caleb or Allen. He rubbed a little of his musky pre-cum on her lips before sliding it between her parted lips.

Ethan began breathing hard as he watched his cock slowly slide into Lily's mouth. Lily didn't know what she was supposed to do. She only knew she loved the taste of Ethan. Moaning around his cock, she wanted to taste more. The combination of Allen sliding in and out of her wet pussy and Ethan sliding in and out of her mouth gave her so much pleasure she felt she was going to explode from all the feelings they were creating inside her.

Her world shattered when Caleb leaned over and pinched her clit. She would have pulled Ethan out of her mouth if it hadn't been for the second hard slap to her ass. Screaming out her orgasm around Ethan's cock she closed her eyes as the orgasm swept through her body, tightening the walls of her pussy so tight Allen jerked in response and yelled out his release, pouring his seed deep inside her.

Ethan pumped his cock faster and faster into her mouth before gripping her hair on each side of her face and releasing his seed down her throat. Lily swallowed as fast as she could, drinking Ethan's heady juice down until there was nothing left. She moaned as Ethan pulled his cock out of her mouth. She felt empty without him. She cried out loudly when Allen slowly pulled his cock out of her pussy. Collapsing on the bed, she felt like all the bones in her body had melted. Caleb gently rolled her over while Allen took her shoes off.

"Come on, baby. Let us clean you up and put you to bed," Ethan murmured gently while he brushed her hair away from her eyes.

Allen left for a moment, and Lily heard the bathtub filling up. Lily didn't want to go anywhere. She wanted to stay wrapped in their arms, holding her safe and secure where she never had to think about the future.

The men bathed Lily and laid her back in the master bedroom bed. Allen stayed with her when she had protested she needed to clean up the kitchen. Ethan and Caleb had hushed her and said they would take care of it. Lily didn't have the strength to protest too much, especially when Allen pulled her into his arms and held her tight against his hard length.

"She's still scared," Ethan said quietly as he covered the casserole up and put it back in the refrigerator.

"I know. We have to find out why she thinks she won't be able to stay," Caleb said as he sat down at the clean table.

"What do you think she meant when she said she wanted to spend what time she had with us?" Caleb asked. A sudden thought popped into his head. It twisted his insides to the point he almost doubled over. "You don't think she's sick, do you? That she might be dying?" Caleb whispered his fear, almost afraid if he said it out loud that would make it be true.

Ethan felt the blood drain from his face at the thought of Lily dying from some illness. Clutching the countertop with both hands, his knuckles stood out white against his tanned skin. "Aw, shit. I hope not. Oh, God. I never even thought of that."

Allen walked quietly into the kitchen. "Never thought of what?" he asked, going to the refrigerator to pull out the milk.

"Why the fuck aren't you with Lily?" Caleb asked, glaring at his brother's bare back.

Allen looked up from pouring the milk. "She's sleeping. I wanted a drink. I also wanted to talk to you guys about what we are going to do to make sure she stays. I don't want her thinking she is only going to be here for a short time. So, what was it you never thought?"

Ethan looked at Caleb before replying slowly, "We were trying to think of why she keeps thinking she will only be here for a short time. Caleb wondered if she knows there is a reason she can't stay."

"Like what? A family member needing her? We know she has never been with another man, so a forgotten husband is out of the question. What other reason would she have?" Allen asked as he drained his glass of milk.

Caleb looked at Allen before he finally answered him, "What if she's sick? Dying? What if she knows and doesn't want us to know?"

Allen felt like someone had just cold cocked him. Staggering to sit in one of the chairs at the table, he sat looking wildly from one brother to the other. "Shit. Goddammit, no! Do you hear me? Fucking *no*," Allen started shaking. He fucking wasn't going to lose her. He looked up with determination shining from his eyes. "Make an appointment in town with Doc

Harley. I want him to check her out from head to toe. You're friends with him, Ethan. You fucking tell him you want her checked out from head to toe."

Ethan looked at Caleb, who was nodding his head in agreement. "He should check her out anyway. None of us used protection. Lily could be pregnant even now. If there is a chance she is and it could harm her, I want to know. Our first duty is to make sure she is healthy."

Each of the men sat in silence. The thought of Lily rounded with their child was something they would all love to see, but not if it meant endangering her. Each one fought the demon of fear that something was wrong with Lily.

A noise at the door of the kitchen had all three men looking up. Standing holding onto the doorframe was Lily. She was biting her lower lip and looking around uncertainly. Dressed in one of Caleb's old flannel shirts that went almost down to her knees and nothing else she looked beautiful to all three of them. Her long dark brown hair was disheveled from their lovemaking and from lying down. She ran her hand down her thigh.

"Is everything okay?" she asked tentatively.

She didn't know what was wrong, but she could feel the tension in the room. Her eyes suddenly filled with tears. Did they regret making love to her? Did they want her to choose one of them over the other? If so, she couldn't do it. She wouldn't do it. She loved all three of them so much.

Ethan pushed away from the counter where he had been standing. "Nothing's wrong, baby. What are you doing up? You should be resting." He pulled her against his warm body, holding her close while he ran his hands down her back. He closed his eyes as he inhaled her sweet scent. He was calling Doc first thing in the morning, Thanksgiving be damned. He had to know she wasn't ill.

"I was cold." Lily looked at Allen. "I missed you." Looking at Ethan and Caleb. "I missed all of you," she added quietly.

Caleb and Allen rose out of their seats and came around to Lily and ran their hands over her. "We'll always be here. One of us will always be with you, Lily. At all times," Caleb said softly as Ethan and Allen nodded in agreement.

"Caleb, why don't you and Allen take her back upstairs. I'll be up later. I have a few things I need to do before I come to bed," Ethan said slowly, releasing

Lily into Caleb's arms. He kissed Lily gently before he turned to head down the hall. He wanted to find out as much as he could about Lily. The first place he was going to start was with his aunt. He wanted to know everything Maggie knew about Lily.

Lily sighed as Caleb lifted her gently into his arms. "Helen is coming over early tomorrow so she can help me with Thanksgiving dinner," Lily said with a yawn, wrapping her arms around Caleb's neck and snuggling her face into his shoulder.

"Then I guess we need to get you to bed," Allen said teasingly, looking over her head to Caleb.

An unspoken message went through both men. They would not leave Lily alone, ever again. She was theirs now and forever, and they would move heaven and hell if they had to in order to protect her.

Chapter 9

Lily hummed along with the music she had playing as she prepared the turkey to go into the oven. Helen had come over an hour before with Clive and was busy making pies. They had laughed and hugged each other as they got started. The men were teasing them that it was going to be hard to stay out of the kitchen with all the good smells coming out of it.

"So, how was your night last night?" Helen teased.

Lily blushed a bright pink, but she couldn't keep the smile from lighting her face. Glancing up briefly into Helen's twinkling eyes, she burst out. "Wonderful, awesome, incredible, unbelievable."

"What's unbelievable?" Allen asked as he walked into the kitchen. Coming up behind Lily, he wrapped his arms around her waist. Tilting her head back, he gave her a deep kiss.

"You are," Lily said huskily. Clearing her throat, she said. "Now, what are you doing in here? You know Helen and I banned all you men from the kitchen until the food was done."

"I missed you," Allen said softly. "You better get used to it, Lily. I need your touch and kisses regularly."

Lily laughed twisting in Allen's arms. "I love you, Allen. So much." She leaned into his arms and gave him another kiss. "Now, out with you before Helen thinks you are here to help."

Allen laughed and swatted Lily on the ass before heading out the back door. Less than an hour later, Ethan came into the kitchen while Lily had her hands covered in flour from making the yeast rolls. Sliding his hands down her sides, he kissed Lily's neck as she tried shooing him away. Flour went everywhere when he bit down on her shoulder, and she jerked with a squeal.

Helen finally had enough of the distractions when Caleb came in thirty minutes later, pulling Lily down onto his lap as he sat down in one of the kitchen chairs. Tilting her back so she was lying in his arms, he gave her a kiss that left her flushed and breathless.

"Enough!" Helen yelled. "You boys get on outta here before I take a spoon to your asses."

Both Caleb and Lily turned shocked eyes on Helen. Caleb laughed. "You owe Lily twenty-five cents, Helen."

"I'll pay her a damn dollar if it gets you boys out of our hair long enough to get Thanksgiving dinner on the table. At the rate we're going it'll be next year before everything is done," Helen said with a stern face. Her hands on her hips showed she meant business.

Caleb stood up, holding Lily in front of him. He leaned over and gave her another kiss. "Ouch!" He jumped just as Lily heard a loud whack. Caleb rubbed his ass where Helen had smacked it with a large wooden spoon. "I'm leaving, I'm leaving."

Lily laughed as she watched Helen move after Caleb, threatening him with the spoon as she said. "And you tell your brothers Lily's off-limits until after dinner. Then you can have her back."

Caleb headed out to the barn rubbing his ass. Ed and Clive raised their eyebrows in question. "Your wife has a mean streak in her, Clive. She's wicked with a wooden spoon," Caleb muttered.

Ed chuckled while Clive shook his head. "She musta broken two dozen of those things on the boys' butts as they were growing up. Got so bad they started hiding them."

"I can understand why," Caleb replied. "Where's Allen and Ethan?"

"They were in the barn. I think they're brewing up a surprise for Lily after dinner," Ed said. "A couple of weeks back, I found the old sleigh you boys had when you were kids in the barn over at the old homestead. I brought it over thinking it would be fun to fix it up for taking Clive's grandkids sleighing. Brad trained Audrey to pull a buggy so I thought we could use him."

Audrey was a gray gelding they had bought two years ago. Brad had been working with him on pulling a buggy for local hay rides and such. It was also good to have a horse to pull a wagon if they needed supplies where a four-wheel vehicle couldn't get.

Caleb grinned and nodded. Walking into the dim interior of the barn, he heard his brothers talking in the back. He walked up and leaned against the wall. "Wow. Ed did a great job. It looks brand new."

"Yeah. We're going to take Lily for a ride after dinner," Allen said with an excited grin. "Helen is going to pack up some hot chocolate and cups for us. Ethan already has some quilts ready in the office. We didn't want her to know."

Caleb grinned. "I'm in. Did you get a hold of Maggie last night?"

Ethan nodded with a grim smile. "She couldn't tell me much. Seems Lily came into town on a bus. Only when I checked the bus schedule, there were no buses the day Lily arrived. She said Lily told her her parents were dead and she had no other family. Seems Lily would work for a while and when the families no longer needed her she would leave. Maggie couldn't tell me anymore."

Caleb stared off into the distance before he commented. "So, all we know is that Lily appeared in town on a bus that doesn't exist and she might not have any family."

Allen asked curiously, "Do we even know how old she is?" He flushed a little as he looked at his two brothers. "I don't know about you, but she looks young to me. You don't think she might be a teenage runaway, do you?"

Caleb blanched at the idea. "I hope to God not after the way we made love to her last night."

Ethan shook his head, groaning. "I didn't even think of it. God, what if she is? We need to find out."

Caleb muttered under his breath as he turned to watch Ed and Clive walk into the barn. "Fat lot of good that will do us now. If she's jailbait they are going to bury us under the jail for what we did to her. Shit, just thinking about it gives me a hard-on."

* * *

Dinner was a joyful affair with good food and good friends in abundance. After dinner the guys pitched in and helped clean up the kitchen since the women did all the cooking. Soon everyone was wishing everyone well as they left with a few hidden yawns.

The younger ranch hands who had joined them for Thanksgiving dinner were heading to the bunkhouse to watch football on the large screen television the men had put in the game room for them. Ed said his good-byes, not even trying to hide the big yawn on his face. Clive and Helen left with promises from Helen to be back in a few days to help start on decorating for Christmas.

Lily had just curled up on the couch in the living room, tucking her legs under the thick throw, and was settling down for a nap. She had already sneaked time to play with the kitten in her room before deciding a nap was in order.

She closed her eyes and smiled as she reflected on the day. For the first time in a long time she had felt like she belonged. She felt like she was part of a family, and she loved it.

She moaned in surprise when she felt firm lips kissing her. Opening her mouth to invite the searching tongue in, she knew it was Allen before she even opened her eyes. She knew his taste. Each of the men tasted different. Each of them tasted delicious. Lily wound her arms around Allen's neck, drawing him down closer to her.

Allen pulled back and smiled tenderly down into Lily's upturned face. "We have a surprise for you."

Lily smiled back. "Does it involve a bed?"

Allen grinned. "Minx. Later. Right now I'm going to get you bundled up. Ethan and Caleb are waiting for us outside."

"But, it's cold," Lily groaned. It had started snowing lightly as everyone was leaving. "I was hoping to take a nap."

"You can take a nap later. Come on." Allen pulled Lily into a sitting position and pulled her feet in front of him, sliding her boots on her. Lily couldn't resist leaning down and grabbing Allen's face between her hands.

"I love you, Allen," Lily said softly. "Happy Thanksgiving."

"Happy Thanksgiving, baby." Allen wrapped the heavy quilt around Lily's shoulders and picked her up in his arms. He had just made it to the front door when Caleb came bursting in.

"What's keeping you two?" he demanded.

"I had to convince Lily to wait on her nap." Allen laughed as Lily nuzzled his neck.

Lily let out a cry of delight when she saw the horse and sleigh in front of the house. Her eyes glistened with tears as she remembered sleighing with her parents when she was young. It had been the only way to get into town during the winter from the farm. It brought back so many memories.

Ethan looked at Lily with concern. "Lily, are you okay?"

Lily pulled her face out from Allen's neck where she had hid it to give her time to recover. "Yes. I was just so surprised. Thank you," she said, her voice full of emotion at the memories.

She looked from one brother to the other. How would she ever survive leaving them? She pushed those thoughts away. She had promised herself she would focus on each new day and live it to the fullest.

Caleb climbed up onto the sleigh and reached for Lily as Allen held her up. Allen climbed up to sit on the other side of her. Ethan climbed in last and took the reins. Lily sat patiently between the two men as they made sure she had plenty of covers and was warm enough. With a click of his tongue Ethan guided the horse and sleigh down the drive.

* * *

Lily loved the sleigh ride. They laughed and sang silly songs as they rode over the meadows and down a narrow road.

"Where are we going?" Lily asked excitedly.

"We're taking you to the old homestead. It's where we grew up," Ethan said.

"I thought the house you live in now is where you grew up," Lily exclaimed in surprise.

"No. Mom and the dads built the house we live in now about twenty years ago. They wanted more room for themselves and for us. They were hoping we would marry and give them lots of grandkids."

"Personally, I think the dads wanted more bathrooms," Allen said. "They were tired of trying to share with us. They were the ones to design the bathrooms."

"Here we are. We come here a few times a year to make sure everything is still in good repair. Even though no one is living here right now, we maintain it just in case one of the ranch hands has a family and needs a place to live," Ethan said, climbing down from the sleigh.

"We came here a few weeks ago, and the house was in pretty good repair, but the barn needed some work," Caleb said, holding his arms open as he helped Lily down.

"Can I take a look around?" Lily asked curiously, looking at the two-story house. It wasn't nearly as big as the home the men lived in now, but it had a character all its own.

"Yeah. We need to look around the barn to see what needs to be done."

"I want to look around the house. I'll meet you guys in the barn in a few minutes," Lily said, already moving toward the house. The men just grinned at each other before nodding and turning to walk around the barn.

Chapter 10

Peter Canton looked out the second-story window of the old house with a curse. He'd had to find another place to stay before the townspeople started talking. He followed Lily and the Simmons woman home the day he had seen them in town.

Scouting around, he felt like he had struck pay dirt when he stumbled upon the old abandoned house. He bought a small kerosene heater and some camping gear and moved in. He hid the stuff in the attic during the day when he was scouting out ways to get to Lily.

So far he had been frustrated. She hardly ever left the ranch house, and when she did, she never went anywhere alone. Usually she was with the Simmons woman, but any other time she had been with one of the men.

He was growing more impatient. He had limited resources and couldn't afford to stay much longer. He was going to have to make his move soon, otherwise he took the chance of losing her again. He might never have another chance.

He watched as the men disappeared into the barn while Lily walked toward the house. Now might be the perfect opportunity. He had his car hidden not too far from here. If he could disable her and steal her away there would be no way the men could chase him with a horse and sleigh. Pulling away from the window, he quietly moved down the stairs and hid.

* * *

Lily ran her hand over the railing as she walked up onto the covered porch. The house had to be a hundred years old, but it was in wonderful repair. She smiled as she saw the men's names carved into the wood near the steps.

Someone had been naughty when they were bored, she thought in amusement. Walking to the front door, she hadn't expected it to be unlocked. Turning the knob, she walked into what had to be the living room. It was a large room with a fireplace on one wall and led to what looked like a dining area. She saw a set of stairs leading to the second floor and grinned as she thought about how often they probably got in trouble for sliding down the railing.

She walked slowly up the stairs and looked in all the rooms. There were four bedrooms upstairs, but only two small bathrooms. She laughed when she thought about the bathrooms each of the men had in their bedrooms at the main house. Both bathrooms here could fit in just one of those with room to spare.

She walked down the stairs and moved into the kitchen. She closed her eyes as she imagined cooking dinner every night for her husbands and children.

Lily jerked in surprise when she felt cold metal pressing into her side. "Not a sound. I would hate to have to kill those men out there. Do you understand?"

Lily nodded stiffly.

"Do you have any idea how long I've been looking for you?" The voice asked in an excited whisper.

All Lily could do was shake her head no. "What do you want?" Lily asked, frightened.

"I want what you have, Lily. I want immortality," the voice whispered.

Before Lily could reply, she felt something hard hit her in the back of the head, and everything went black.

* * *

"I don't think it will be too much to get it back in shape. That tree branch did a number, but we have everything we need at the main house to fix it. I'll talk to Ed about bringing a couple of guys over in the next couple of weeks to work on it," Ethan said, looking at the hole in the roof of the barn.

Caleb looked around. "Yeah. Maybe we can extend the loft area. This would be a good place to store some of the extra hay during the winter months."

Allen looked uneasily over his shoulder again. "Where's Lily? She should have been here by now."

Ethan laughed. "She is probably finding all the places we carved our initials into the wood before mom tore us a new one."

Caleb laughed, adding. "Yeah. She gave the dads hell for months after they bought us those pocket knives."

Allen shivered again. "Yeah, well, I don't like her being out of my sight for so long. I'll meet you guys up at the house."

"Okay, we'll be there in a few minutes."

Allen strode out of the barn and headed toward the house. He didn't know why, but he felt uneasy. "Lily!" he yelled as he took the steps up to the front door two at a time. "Lily, where are you?"

Pushing the door open, he stood a moment listening. The house was too quiet. Had she fallen? He should never have let her come up here alone. "Lily, answer me now."

Running up the stairs, he searched the upstairs rooms. Finding nothing, he practically jumped down the stairs, grabbing the doorframe and swinging into the kitchen. Frowning, he glanced frantically around.

"Lily, dammit, answer me." Still no response.

He was beginning to sweat now as panic set in. As he turned he noticed something on the floor. Bending he picked up one of Lily's gloves. As he straightened, he noticed a red spot on the floor not far from it. Kneeling down, he took off his glove, and using a finger touched the red stain. His finger came away smeared with blood.

"Ethan! Caleb!" Allen roared, running for the front door.

Both men heard Allen's roar of rage and came out of the barn running like the hounds of hell were on their heels. "What is it? Where's Lily?" Ethan demanded.

Allen held out his hands so his brothers could see her glove in one hand and blood on the other. Allen's eyes had grown hard and cold. He was no longer their brother, but a Special Forces officer set to kill.

"Spread out. Look for tracks. If Lily is unconscious, whoever has her will be moving slow through the snow."

The men spread out, taking each side of the house looking at the snow for telltale tracks. If they found none, they knew she would still be in the house. They met at the back door, staring at the tracks. Suddenly the silence was shattered by the sound of a car trying to start. Allen took off running full blast.

He yelled over his shoulder, "Ethan, get the sleigh."

Caleb ran, following Allen through the woods while Ethan went back for the sleigh. Allen paused as he heard the sound of an engine revving up. He knew there was only one road out.

Swerving, he ran for a small hill just in time to see a car fishtailing as the wheels hit an icy spot. Pulling free the knife he kept strapped to his waist, he half ran, half slid down the hill, dodging trees and trying to get to the car before the tires had a good chance to grip. He was coming up on the passenger side. Through the window he could see Lily's pale face, her eyes closed.

Rage like he had never felt before, even during his captivity, ran through his body. His eyes narrowed in on the driver. Suddenly, he yelled out for Caleb to take cover. The driver had lowered the passenger window and opened fire with a handgun.

Allen cursed under his breath as he dove for cover under a fallen log. Bark flew up around his head, small bits of it biting into the skin of his cheek. By the time he was able to look up again the car had straightened out and was moving down the road.

Caleb ran up next to him. "You okay?"

"Shit. Let's move. If we can get through the woods over the next rise the road curves back around and we can catch him. He has Lily. She wasn't moving. If that son of a bitch has hurt her, I'm gonna kill him," Allen snarled as he pushed up and over the log.

Crossing the road, both men headed up the next rise. The road curved around on itself about a quarter mile down before it crossed the river. If they could get there first they might be able to stop the car somehow and get Lily out. He didn't know how, but he wasn't giving up.

Clawing at the slick ground for traction, the men scrambled, on all fours at times, to reach the top. From the rise they could see the car's taillights as the man who grabbed Lily hit the brakes to make a sharp turn.

"Let's go," Allen said, sliding down the rise and running as fast as he could through the thick snow.

* * *

Lily moaned softly. She came awake suddenly when she realized she couldn't move her hands separately. They were tied together with what looked like a thick plastic zip tie.

Struggling to sit up, she shivered as the cold air coming in through the passenger window hit her. Looking in horror at the man driving, she shrank as far away from him as she could. The man glanced at her before focusing on the road again.

"Don't try anything. I might not be able to kill you, but I sure as hell can hurt you. Do you understand me?" he said in a harsh voice. "I've looked for you for too many years to let you go now."

"Why?" Lily asked in a small voice. "Why have you looked for me? What do you want with me?"

The man looked at Lily again. "I know about you. I want what you have."

Lily shivered violently. "I don't know what you are talking about. What do you know about me? What could I possibly have that you would want enough to hurt me for?"

"You don't understand. I want what you have enough to kill for it. I'll kill every fucking man, woman, or child you know to get it," he said in a hard voice.

Lily trembled as she listened to him. She believed him. God help her, she believed he would kill the people she loved to get something she was supposed to have. "Please. Don't hurt anyone. I'll give you whatever you want. I promise. Whatever I'm supposed to have that you want, you can have it. It isn't worth killing over."

"You're wrong. It is. There are even more powerful men than me who would kill for it if they knew about it," the man's cold voice replied harshly.

"What is it? You can have it," Lily begged.

"Immortality," the man said. "I want to live forever."

Lily was confused. He thought she was immortal? "I don't understand. How can I help you with being immortal?"

"I know about you, Lily O'Donnell. You were born May 23, 1901. They thought you died with your mother in 1919, but you didn't. Your body was never found. I have other dates where you've appeared and supposedly died. Only you didn't. They never found your body to bury, did they?"

Lily began trembling. It had started. It was the beginning of the end. She would soon have to leave again. Looking down at her trembling hands she clutched them together.

Instead of denying it, Lily looked up at the man driving. "How did you find out?"

The man smirked. He had been expecting her to deny it and was more than prepared to show her the evidence, not to mention making her pay for lying to him. "The Internet."

Never before had anyone realized she was the same Lily. She should have known it could happen with the invention of the Internet. "I'm not immortal."

The man backhanded Lily across the face. Lily gasped as she placed her fingers to her mouth, coming away with blood. "Don't fucking lie to me. Every time you lie to me or withhold information, you'll get more of that."

Lily didn't say anything else. She had to get away from him. He was insane. She watched as they rounded another curve in the gravel road before noticing a small, narrow bridge coming up.

He would have to slow down to cross it. It would be too dangerous otherwise. He would also have to stay focused on the road instead of her. If she could manage to open the door, she could fling herself out over the side of the bridge. It didn't look like it was too far a drop. If the river was frozen, she would be able to take cover under the bridge. He wouldn't be able to get to her without jumping out. It would be more difficult with the steering wheel.

Holding her hands to her face as if she were still hurting from the blow he had given her, she let her eyes drift down to the controls on the door. She could unlock and open the door at the same time if she was lucky. Sobbing softly, she held her breath as they came to the narrow bridge. When they were halfway across, Lily reached frantically for the lock and door handle, pushing with all her might against the door as she flung herself out of it and over the edge of the bridge.

For a moment she was free-falling through the air before she landed hard on the ice-covered river. She gasped as pain exploded through her when she hit the hard ice. She had landed on her side. Before she had a chance to move, the ice cracked under her, and she fell through to the icy water below.

She swallowed a mouthful of water as her body reacted to the cold water. Clawing at the ice, she banged against it with her tied fists as she was swept under the ice, away from the hole where she had fallen through. She kicked desperately with her feet, trying to find a hold that would allow her to pull herself back to the light, but the cold was already working against her.

She could feel herself starting to lose consciousness. Her last thought before she did was that she didn't want to leave the men she loved. She had just found them.

* * *

Allen and Caleb had made it down the side of the hill before the car had made the sharp curve and were waiting for it on the other side of the bridge. They knew the driver would have to slow down and planned on charging the car right after the driver crossed it. They had each taken up a different side of the road. Allen would go after the driver while Caleb pulled Lily from the car and to safety.

They waited patiently as the car reached the bridge and slowed to a crawl. The bridge was barely wide enough for a car and was hazardous under the best of conditions. Their dads had planned to replace it a long time ago, but instead had made a new road which ran through the woods and came out at the new house.

Now as they waited, they were thankful the old bridge was still there. Both men tensed as the car stopped suddenly, halfway across. They heard a yell at the same time the passenger door flew open and a body went sailing off the bridge to land hard on the icy river below. The driver cursed as there was no way for him to open his door and get out without falling also.

Both men stared in horror as Lily's body dropped through the air to land with a thud under the bridge.

As both men began climbing down the side of the bank to the river they heard the crack of the ice followed by a cry before everything went silent except for the sound of the car engine running. The driver noticed the men coming out of the woods and gunned the engine, moving at a reckless speed over the bridge.

* * *

Peter slammed his fist against the dashboard. The bitch had tricked him into thinking she was weak and fragile. He couldn't stop now. He had noticed the other man coming up behind him on the road in the horse and sleigh. If the bitch survived the fall, he would have another chance at her. He knew she wouldn't tell the men about who or what she was. He would be considered some homeless guy whom she had chanced upon, and sooner or later they would let their guard down. When they did, he would be there.

Fishtailing as he finished crossing the bridge, he drove recklessly down the road until he reached the highway. There was no way to identify him as he was wearing dark glasses and a hat. He had worn gloves everywhere thanks to the damn cold weather. He would dump the car, get another one, shave and change. He would not underestimate the bitch next time. He would make sure she was too hurt to try to escape from him.

Allen ran along the bank to where Lily had fallen through the ice, looking desperately around under the ice. He pulled off his jacket and slid through the hole, swimming along with the current under the ice. He had to trust Caleb would follow him until he found Lily. If not, he didn't give a damn. If Lily didn't make it, he didn't give a shit if he did.

Pulling himself along, he swept his hands out. His left hand brushed something. Struggling against the current, he reached again and felt Lily's arms floating lifelessly. He pulled her body toward his and banged on the ice with his fist.

Caleb had watched as Allen had slipped into the icy hell and followed him as he swam just under the surface of the frozen river. The moment he heard Allen banging on the ice, he slammed the sharp end of his knife through the ice, breaking it.

Pulling desperately at the edges, he ignored the sharp edges cutting into his hands as he tried frantically to save his brother and the woman he loved. As soon as he had an opening large enough, he reached down and pulled on Allen's shirt.

Ethan had pulled up onto the end of the bridge. His heart was in his throat as he had watched the nightmare unfold before his eyes. He had engaged the brake on the sleigh and slid down the opposite side of the bank, running recklessly across the ice trying to get to Caleb. He slid to a stop just as Caleb was pulling Allen up by the back of his shirt.

Allen was shivering uncontrollably. "Forget… about me. Take Lily. Get her… out of this… shit," he stammered.

Caleb grabbed Lily's arms and pulled her out of the water while Ethan helped Allen up and over the edge. Caleb was frantically working on Lily.

"She's not breathing. Dammit, she's not breathing." Caleb pressed on Lily's chest, then moved to blow air into her mouth. He kept going back and forth. "Breathe, damn you. Breathe, you hear me, Lily? I won't let you die. Dammit, you fucking breathe."

Allen lay there shivering as he watched Caleb work on Lily. He felt numb. They couldn't lose her. They had so much to live for. They had just found each other.

Ethan slid on his knees to where Lily was lying. "Lily, listen to me, baby. You've got to breathe for us. We need you. Allen, Caleb, and I. We need you. Please, baby. Please. Breathe for us. You can do it." He ran his trembling hands over her cold face. "Where's the fucking helicopter. I called in what happened. I told Matt our position and told him to send the rescue helicopter just in case."

All three men turned at the same time when they heard the soft cough come from Lily followed by another one. A moment later she rolled over and threw up river water on the ice and gasped for breath. Caleb and Ethan reached for her at the same time and helped her roll back onto her back. It tore them up as they watched her struggle for another breath. Slowly, she opened her eyes.

"C-c-c-old. So c-c-cold," Lily muttered, shivering violently.

Ethan took off his jacket. He cut the plastic ties on Lily's wrists before he sat her up partway and pulled her wet shirt off, sliding her arms into his warm jacket. At the same time the sound of sirens and a helicopter filled the air above the river.

Caleb ran down to where Allen's jacket was and picked it up. Racing back to his brother he shoved out of his jacket and helped Allen remove his wet shirt. Allen couldn't feel his fingers anymore and had to let his brother undo the buttons for him.

He shook violently as Caleb pulled the jacket around him. The warmth felt like thousands of needles against his icy skin. Nodding his thanks, since he couldn't get his frozen vocal cords to work, he struggled to his feet as the sheriff, Matt Holden, and a few of his deputies walked cautiously out onto the ice.

"What the hell is going on?" Matt barked out. "Shit. Get them to the helicopter." He turned and nodded at two of his deputies.

"I'll carry Lily," Ethan said. "Caleb, you go with them too. You need to get your hands looked at."

Ethan picked up Lily's shivering body. She was only partially conscious, and he was worried about her. He had noticed a dark bruise in the form of a handprint forming on her left cheek and how her lip was swollen. He bit down the dark rage eating at him. He needed to keep his head until he was sure his brothers and Lily were going to be all right.

Struggling up the side of the bank, Ethan reluctantly handed Lily over to the paramedics. All too soon, the helicopter taking his two brothers and Lily to the hospital in Boulder Flats was just a faint speck in the sky.

"What's going on, Ethan?" Matt asked.

Ethan looked at the sheriff. They were the same age and had grown up together. "We went to the old homestead to check out some damage to the barn. We wanted to show Lily where we had grown up." Nodding toward the horse and sleigh still on the other side of the bridge he turned back to look at Matt. "Caleb, Allen, and I were in the barn talking about the repairs. Lily wanted to see the house. We were going to join her after we had determined what needed to be done. When Allen went into the house, he called for Lily and didn't get an answer. He found her glove and some blood on the floor in the kitchen. We tracked the bastard who had taken her. Allen and Caleb went ahead while I brought up the rear with the sleigh in case we needed it. Dammit, she was only out of our sight for fifteen, maybe twenty minutes, tops. How could some bastard do this to her?" Ethan said, a shudder running through his tall frame.

"Do you have any idea who it could be?" Matt asked.

"No. I've never seen the car before. Allen and Caleb saw more of it than I did. I know whoever was driving was armed. I heard him shooting at Allen and Caleb."

"How did the woman, Lily, escape?" Matt asked as they walked across the bridge.

"She jumped from the car when it was halfway across the bridge. She must have figured he would have to slow down. God, Matt, I've never been so scared in all my life when I saw her falling from the bridge. She hit the ice hard, and it broke, sweeping her under it. Allen jumped in after her." Ethan turned pleading eyes toward the man walking next to him. "We can't lose her, Matt. We can't lose her."

Matt stopped and stared at the man he had known his whole life. Never before had he seen Ethan lose control of his emotions. Even when they were kids, he had always been the calm, steady, rational one of the group. The man standing before him now looked close to shattering into a million pieces.

"Who is the woman? I've never seen her before. She looks young," Matt asked.

"Her name is Lily." Ethan gave a self-depreciative laugh. "I don't even know her last name. Can you believe it? I love her more than life itself, and I don't even know her last name or how old she is. We were going to ask her tonight. Maggie hired her a little over a month ago to be our housekeeper. She's turned our world upside down and inside out."

"Let's get you back to the house. I'll drive you into town. I want to see how the others are doing and post some guards on Lily to make sure the bastard who took her doesn't get another chance. I'll have Trace and Brent go over to the old homestead and comb it. Those two could track a lizard in the desert. If anyone can find out who the bastard is or his M.O., those two can. I'd like to meet this girl who has the Cunnings men so torn up."

Ethan nodded as he climbed into the sleigh. Releasing the brake, he turned Audrey around and slapped the reins. Matt watched as Ethan took off across the meadow. He wanted to know more about this girl who had stolen his friend's heart, and from the looks of it, the hearts of his brothers. Boulder Flats was a close-knit community. They didn't appreciate anyone coming in and harming someone, especially one of their women. Sometimes they had even resorted to the law of the west.

He couldn't help but wonder as he walked back to his car how could a man, or men, fall in love with someone and not even know how old she was or what her last name was. Shaking his head, he turned off the flashing lights and drove carefully over the bridge, pausing at the spot where Lily had thrown herself out of the car.

It was a hell of a long way down. It was amazing she had survived the fall much less the time she was trapped under the ice. Someone must have been looking out for that little girl, he thought.

Chapter 11

Lily faded in and out of consciousness over the next three days. She had developed a mild case of pneumonia and had severe bruising on her hip and leg where she had landed on the ice. She also had a shallow cut on the back of her head where she had been hit, as well as bruising from where her assailant had hit her across the face.

Allen had been released after he had taken a hot shower and changed into some dry clothes. The nurse had pumped him full of hot coffee to help ward off the chills. Caleb's hands were treated. He needed stitches for one particularly bad cut, but otherwise he was going to be fine. It was Lily they were worried about. She had never fully regained consciousness and was unable to answer any questions about her abduction.

All three men stayed at her side, growling whenever the doctor or nurse came in to suggest they go home to get some rest. After the first night, Ethan's friend, Doc Harley, had a couple of cots and blankets sent up with instructions if the men didn't take turns getting some rest, he was going to give them each a sedative to help them sleep whether they wanted it or not.

Helen, Clive, and Ed came daily to spend time with Lily. Even Brad and Harold came in to see how she was doing, telling her they missed her cooking. Helen had reassured Lily that she was taking care of the kitten so Lily didn't need to worry about it. Clive had taken a liking to the little bugger and was spoiling it rotten.

"Why won't she wake up?" Allen asked, holding Lily's pale hand in his. "I want to see her eyes. I need to tell her I love her."

"Harley said she'll wake up when she's ready. She's been through a lot. He said sometimes it just takes time for someone who has gone through a traumatic event to heal. He said the best thing we can do is talk to her. Let her know she is safe and that we love her," Ethan said quietly. He had pulled a chair up near the head of the bed and was running his hand over her face and hair. He didn't think he would ever get enough of touching her.

"Well, I don't fucking like it," Caleb growled from the window. "She should have woken up by now." Walking over and picking up Lily's other hand, he rubbed his thumb back and forth. "Lily, you hear me? You fucking wake up right now. Enough of this shit. You need to open those beautiful eyes of yours and tell us you love us. Do you fucking hear me?" Ethan and Allen frowned in disapproval at Caleb.

"Caleb, you owe me a dollar," a soft voice whispered.

Lily struggled to find her way back to consciousness. She hurt all over. From the top of her head down to the tips of her toes, she felt like she had been beaten, run over, and put through a grinder all at the same time.

She could feel her men in the room with her and wanted to be with them, but she just couldn't seem to get her body to cooperate. Focusing on moving her lips first, she knew she had to respond to Caleb before Allen and Ethan tore into him. Now she focused on trying to work her eyelids. If she could just convince them to open a little, she felt like she could work at getting the rest later.

Lily's eyelids slowly lifted with great effort. She stared, blurry-eyed, up at the ceiling with a frown. She didn't remember any of the rooms in the main house having a ceiling like this. It was too much effort to turn her head. She was just about to give up and close her eyes again when Caleb's face came into focus above her.

"Don't you fu—" Caleb began, before starting over. "Don't you close those beautiful blue eyes yet, sweetheart."

Lily frowned as she let her eyes move around. Ethan's face slowly came into focus behind Caleb's. "Where am I?" she whispered hoarsely.

Was that her voice? Why did her throat hurt so bad? She was having a hard time keeping her eyes open.

"You're in the hospital, baby," Ethan said. "You've had us scared."

"Allen?" Lily asked.

"I'm here, baby," Allen said as he squeezed her hand.

Lily turned her head slowly toward him. "I thought it was time for me to go again," Lily said sleepily. "I love you. All of you. So very much. I don't have much time left. I'm so sorry. I didn't want to hurt you. I didn't want to…" Lily faded back to a peaceful sleep, unable to stay awake any longer.

Helen stood in the doorway of the hospital room. She was holding a tattered journal in her arms, silent tears sliding down her cheeks. Wiping them away, she moved into the room, walking over to Ethan.

"Lily asked me to give this to you if something should happen to her. I don't know if this is what she meant, but I think you should read it. I know I shouldn't have, but I couldn't help myself after a copy of an old newspaper article fell out."

Ethan took the journal from Helen with a sense of foreboding. He knew whatever was in the journal would answer many of the questions he and his brothers had about Lily. He just didn't know if it was important any longer.

Helen looked at Lily and smiled sadly. "She's an incredible young lady who deserves to be loved." Walking over, she leaned down and kissed Lily's forehead before turning and walking to the door. "I'll tell the nurses not to disturb you. You'll need time to absorb what you are going to learn and decide if you can accept what Lily has to offer you."

Allen, Caleb, and Ethan remained silent as Helen closed the door quietly behind her. Ethan walked over to the corner chair and turned on the light. Sitting down, he opened the journal and gasped when he read the inscription. Clearing his throat, he looked at his brothers with tears in his eyes.

"You might want to sit down," Ethan said in a somber voice. Clearing his throat, Ethan began reading.

> *To our beloved daughter, may you find happiness. Happy 16th birthday, Lily. Love, Momma and Da. Dated: May 23, 1917.*

Ethan cleared his throat again before picking up the picture under the caption. He handed it gently to Allen and Caleb. It was a picture of Lily when she was sixteen. Only, Lily and her parents were dressed in old-fashioned clothing similar to the pictures people had taken when they visited old ghost towns. It was obvious this picture had been taken long ago. Ethan continued reading.

> *May 23, 1917*

> *Today was my 16th birthday. Momma and Da gave me a journal so I could write about all the exciting things they say will happen in my life. Da gave me a beautiful red ribbon and Momma braided it into my hair. Da is going to take Momma and me to town in the wagon. There is supposed to be some type of festival, and Momma begged Da to take us. I am so excited.*

> *June 20, 1917*

James Butler came around again today. Da threatened him with the shotgun. He asked Da for my hand in marriage. The man scares me. Da told him to leave and not come back. Da told me not to worry. I know some of the girls get married this young, but I don't want to. I want to travel the world. Momma tells me stories every night of all the wonders to be found. She talks about what it was like in Ireland before her and Da came to America. I want to see the world before I settle down with someone who loves me the way Da loves Momma.

July 10, 1917

I wish I could write more and more often. I don't want to use up all the pages. I want to save some for when I travel so I can record all my adventures. Amy Mullins' family is moving to Texas. She promised she would write and tell me about it. Oh, but to go somewhere else.

September 14, 1917

Today my heart broke. My beautiful Da was killed in an accident. At least the sheriff said it was an accident. He was working with James Butler at the Peterson's place. Butler claims Da fell off the roof of the barn. My Da could climb anything and not fall. I suspect Butler had something to do with it, but the sheriff won't listen. I don't know what Momma and I will do. The farm is all we have left besides each other. Da, if you are in heaven, please help Momma and me. I miss you so much already. Love always, your faithful daughter, Lily.

February 16, 1918

It has been a hard winter. Momma had to sell most of the livestock. Many of the towns' folks have become very ill. Some have died. I'm scared for Momma. She hasn't been well since Da died. I'm afraid I might lose her, and then I won't have anyone. James Butler keeps coming by but Momma won't give the man the time of day. She sends him away before he even gets off his horse. If the spring doesn't come soon I fear our food supplies will run dangerously low. Da, if you can hear me, please take care of Momma. She misses you so much, as do I. Love always, your faithful daughter, Lily.

June 15, 1918

I've had to pick up some housekeeping work with the Petersons to help buy food. The garden isn't producing as much as we would like. Mr. Marshall at the General Store has agreed to purchase some of our vegetables to sell at his store. I'll drop it off once a week when I go to clean the Peterson's. James Butler hasn't been around much lately, thank goodness. Momma is still weak and needs me. I do what I can around the farm. We are down to just old Gladys, the mule, and Trudy, the milk cow, plus a handful of chickens. Thank goodness for the chickens, their eggs have been a blessing. Some nights I get so hungry, but I know I shouldn't eat the food we need to sell. Da, Momma says to say hello. She'll wait for you. I love you too, Da. Love always, your faithful daughter, Lily.

December 24, 1918

A blizzard blew in last night. There is almost an inch of ice on the inside of the windows. I can't write long as we need to save the candles. I just wanted to wish you a Merry Christmas, Da. Love always, your faithful daughter, Lily.

February 23, 1919

James Butler has been coming around again. Two of our chickens have disappeared, and I suspect *he had something to do with it. He is trying to get Momma to marry him, but she won't. She won't ever look at another man. She still grieves for Da. He threatened her. I told her she should tell the sheriff, but she won't. I'll be eighteen soon, and the Petersons have said they would hire me full-time as their housekeeper. The farm is more than what Momma and I can handle. If I get the job, the Petersons said we can move into the cabin near the main house. I'll move Momma there and will be able to take care of her better. Da, I'm worried. Please, if you are looking down on us say a prayer for us. Love always, your faithful daughter, Lily.*

March 4, 1919

Oh, God. Please help us. James Butler caught me alone in our barn today. I was so scared. He grabbed me, and it hurt so bad I screamed. Momma heard me and came running. I know he would have hurt me more if Momma hadn't picked up the pitchfork and threatened him. He told her he was going to marry her and have me too. It was going to be a package deal. He said such awful things Momma and I both cried. Da, if you are there, please keep us safe. I'm so scared. Love always, your faithful daughter, Lily.

April 11, 1919

James Butler came to the house and threatened Momma and me again. He caught me in the barn again and hurt me. Momma came out with the shotgun and warned him away, but I fear he will be back. All our chickens are dead. I found a man's footprint leading away from the coop, and it was right after James Butler hurt me. The sheriff won't listen to me, but I plan on telling him what happened again tomorrow when I go to town. I don't want to go and leave Momma alone, but we need to sell our canned goods. The sheriff said Momma and I needed to move away last time. I know he'll tell us again, but where will we go? We have no family. Please Da, we need you. Love always, your faithful daughter, Lily.

April 12, 1919

I died today. I am so scared. I haven't even had a chance to live and already my life is over. I came home late because of the rain. It took me longer than I expected. I should have stayed home. Maybe Momma and I wouldn't have died if I had stayed home. The mud was so hard to walk through it took me longer than I expected to go to town and back. I wanted to let the sheriff know about the threats James Butler had made last night. I knew something was wrong when the house was dark. Momma always had a light shining for me. I found Momma dead. James Butler had raped and beaten her. He said he was going to do to the same to me. I fought him and ran out the door. If only I could have gotten to the Peterson's place. He caught me down by the river. I fought him off again, but there was nowhere to run. He had me trapped. The river was swollen because of all the rain we were having. I'm so sorry, Momma. I wish I could have saved you. I can't let him do to me what he did to you. May God have mercy on my soul. I would rather face death than have his hands on me. He said I didn't have a choice, but I did. I chose the river.

May 23, 1919

Today would have been my eighteenth birthday. I don't know where I've been for the last month. I know I died. I watched as they buried my beautiful Momma next to Da. At least they are together. I saw the volunteers looking for my body. I called and called to them, but no one ever turned around. I knew I was dead when I tried to stop Mr. Peterson. My hand went right through him, and I saw him shudder. It is strange to know you are dead and can do nothing about it. I feel so alone. Is this the price I must pay for taking my own life? Oh, Momma and Da, I miss you so much.

Oklahoma Press

Wednesday, April 12, 1919

Mother and Daughter Killed By Local Man

The body of a local woman, Maureen O'Donnell, was found beaten and strangled to death. Her daughter, Lily O'Donnell, has not been found, but she is presumed dead. Lily O'Donnell had gone to the local sheriff complaining about threats made by James Butler, a local farmer. It is suspected Butler killed the mother before attacking the daughter and tossing her body in the local river, swollen from the recent rains. Law enforcement officials have arrested Butler after he confessed during a drunken rage. Volunteers continue to search the river for Miss O'Donnell's body. Burial for her mother will be at the Oak Grove Cemetery on April 25, in the year of our Lord 1919 at 2:00 p.m.

Ethan's hands and voice were shaking so bad he had to stop. He looked at the obituary and newspaper article Lily had placed in the journal. He lifted tortured eyes to his brothers as he handed it to them.

"Is it possible?" Allen asked shakily. "This is crazy."

Caleb didn't say anything; he still held the picture of Lily with her parents. The girl in the picture could have been Lily's twin.

"There's more," Ethan said quietly.

Ethan read entry after entry recorded for almost a hundred years. Lily talked about how there were times she just seemed to float through years without really existing. She knew everything that was going on, she was just more of an observer than a participant.

It seemed only when someone called out for help that she existed in the physical plane. Each time, once the person or family had been helped, she would "die" again. She had appeared this time when she heard Maggie's call for help. Her last entry was dated Thanksgiving morning.

November 24, 2010

I spent the day yesterday with Helen. I was so confused and needed someone to talk to. I have never felt the way I do about anyone the way I do about Ethan, Caleb, and Allen. It hurt so much, them not talking to me. I didn't know what to do. I love them with all my heart, but I know I won't be here much longer. Already they are healing and won't need me. I shouldn't let them fall in love with me knowing our time will be so short. I remember the pain of losing Momma and Da. I can't imagine surviving the loss of someone who is the other half of me. Allen told me he loved me. What will happen when I "die" again? I have no control over it. I needed help, and Helen gave me so much more. She made me realize there were no guarantees in life, and I should grab what I can and hold on to it as long as I can. It was funny all the things I was supposed to help Ethan, Caleb, and Allen with were things I had problems with as well. Ethan had trouble enjoying the simple things in life. He was always so worried about everyone else, he forgot about himself. I realized I had done the same thing. Before, I worried about Momma, then all the other families I had to help. I've decided if I am to help Ethan, then I had to realize I needed to help myself. I plan on grabbing hold of life and living it to the fullest every day I am given with my men. Like Caleb, I bottled up my emotions, holding them inside me where they ate away at me. Never again will I hold back. Last night I let my men know I loved them with everything I was. I wanted to scream to the world I loved them all. My last challenge was Allen. My beloved Allen. Like him, I had given up on life. He showed me how much I had to live for. His love broke the wall I had surrounded myself with. For the first time, I want to fight to have a life. To love and be loved. Momma, I wish I could tell you I have found a love like you had with Da. I love my men so very much. If I am given a short time with them so be it. I would rather have had the chance to love them than to have never loved at all. Your faithful daughter, Lily.

Ethan closed the journal. All three of them sat quietly, reflecting on what they had just discovered. They had learned things about Lily they had never expected. Ethan ran his hands over the cover.

Chapter 12

Lily had woken as Ethan had begun reading some of her newer entries. She knew they had her journal. A single tear tracked down the side of her face as she listened to her struggle and subsequent discovery of accepting her unconditional love for them.

Would they feel the same now they knew what she was? Who she was? Would they want to be with her knowing her time with them would be short?

A second tear slid down her cheek, then another and another until uncontrollable sobs shook her fragile body. Her grief could no longer be contained, and she sobbed out all her years of loneliness, pain, and fear.

Strong arms wrapped themselves around her shaking shoulders. Lily felt Caleb's arms as they held her close to his chest. She turned her face into his soft shirt, absorbing his strength.

"Hush, Lily. It will be all right, baby. You'll see. It will be all right," Caleb said as he ran his hands over her hair.

Lily felt the bed dip next to her and felt more hands on her. Running over her hair, her shoulders, her arms. Turning tear-filled eyes toward the three men sitting on the bed next to her, Lily whispered softly, "I love you all so much."

"Lily, it doesn't change anything. You're still ours," Ethan said quietly.

"We love you, Lily. No matter what, we love you," Allen said gently.

Lily turned to look up at Caleb. "Caleb?" Lily looked up uncertainly at Caleb.

"I love you, Lily. Always." Caleb's arms tightened around Lily, and he buried his face in her hair. He shuddered. "I thought we had lost you."

"I did too for a little while," Lily said softly. "What happened? I don't remember very much after I fell through the ice." She shivered again. She didn't know if she would ever feel warm again.

"Allen and I had made it to the other side of the bridge. We were going to attack the man who took you from both sides right before he drove off it. When we saw your body falling from the bridge—" Caleb stopped and took a deep breath. "We should beat your ass for that little stunt."

"Who took you, Lily? Did you know him?" Allen asked. "I couldn't get a good look at him."

Lily shook her head. She was about to answer when a soft knock sounded on the door. Ethan got up and opened it. Matt stood outside the door.

"Is she awake?" he asked quietly. Ethan nodded and opened the door further.

"Lily, this is Matt Holden. He's the sheriff for Boulder Flats," Ethan said. "He needs to ask you some questions."

Lily held the sheriff's gaze for a moment before nodding. "Okay." She couldn't help searching for Allen's and Caleb's hands. She needed them close. She watched as Ethan walked over to the chair by the window and casually slid the journal out of view.

"Lily, can you tell us anything about the man who abducted you?" Matt asked.

Lily shook her head. "I don't know who he was. I had gone to check out the house Allen, Ethan, and Caleb had grown up in while they checked on the barn. When I went into the kitchen, he came up behind me. He hit me with something, and I don't remember anything more until I woke up in his car."

Allen moved to sit on the bed so he could pull Lily into his arms. He hated how she had started shaking again. "It's okay, Lily. Just tell us what you remember."

Lily took a deep breath and sank back against Allen. "He said he wanted something, but I didn't understand what he meant." Lifting her hand to the side of her face, she touched her bruised cheek, "He hit me. He said he was going to hurt me and anyone I loved if I didn't help him." Lily's eyes filled with tears as she remembered the look on the man's face. "I didn't say anything else. I was so afraid. He was insane. I knew I had to get away from him. When I saw the bridge I knew he would have to slow down. I thought if I could jump from the bridge he wouldn't be able to get me. It didn't look as high as it was. Then the ice broke, and I couldn't get out. I don't remember anything else. I'm sorry." Lily closed her eyes, exhausted.

Caleb stood up and brushed a gentle kiss across Lily's forehead. "That's enough, Matt. Lily's exhausted and needs to rest. You can ask more questions later if you need to."

Matt nodded and picked up his hat, walking toward the door with Ethan he turned at the last minute, "I've posted a man here at the hospital to keep an eye on Lily. I know you three won't be leaving her side any time soon, so I feel better. Ethan, if you have a moment I'd like to talk to you out in the hall."

Ethan nodded and looked at his brothers. "I'll be back in a few minutes." Both men nodded. Allen gently laid Lily back down. She had already fallen back asleep.

Matt waited until the door closed before turning to look at Ethan carefully.

"What is it? I don't like being away from her right now for very long," Ethan said impatiently.

"A funny thing happened when I did a search on Lily's name," Matt began.

Ethan looked sharply at Matt. "How could you do that without knowing her last name?"

"Helen told me. I don't think she realized you and your brothers didn't know it. I saw her last night when I went out to check on the evidence Trace and Brent had found." Matt shifted nervously from one foot to the other.

Ethan braced himself. "What did you find?"

"Nothing much at the house. Whoever it was he had standard camping gear. We haven't been able to pull any prints. With the cold weather the bastard probably wore gloves. We are checking to see where the equipment was purchased, to see if we can trace it through a purchase receipt or if a store employee remembers him." Matt looked hard at Ethan before continuing, "What do you know about Lily?"

Ethan's mouth tightened. "My brothers and I know everything we need to know about her. Why?"

"I told you a strange thing happened when I put her name through the system. Seems there have been a number of strange disappearances concerning a girl with her name."

"What does that have to do with Lily?" Ethan asked impatiently, not liking where this was leading.

Matt ran his hand through his hair, looking at the closed door before answering. "This is going to sound crazy, Ethan. I thought I was going nuts at first, but after looking at the girl in that room and looking at the photos I have in my office, I know I'm not. I just don't know how it's possible."

Ethan put his hand on Matt's arm. "Does it matter who she is? All I know is she is here now, and Caleb,

Allen, and I are going to do whatever we can to make sure she stays here with us. You don't have to understand it anymore than we do. Just accept she means everything to us and help us catch the bastard who almost killed her." Matt studied Ethan's face for a moment before letting out a relieved sigh. He really didn't want to have to express his findings out loud. Ethan was right. Nothing mattered, but keeping Lily safe.

Nodding his acceptance, Matt squeezed Ethan's arm. "We'll catch the bastard and keep Lily safe. She is a part of our community. We protect our own."

Ethan smiled his gratitude before turning to go back into the room with Lily and his brothers. "Thanks, Matt."

Chapter 13

Lily was released from the hospital two days later. The men had been adamant she let them carry her everywhere. Her hip and leg still hurt so it was difficult for her to walk without assistance.

Once home, Allen wanted to carry her upstairs, but she begged them to let her lie on the couch. She was tired of being cooped up in a small room, although the master bedroom could in no way be described as small. Ed, Clive, Brad, and Harold all welcomed her home. Clive told her Helen was going to come over later to visit.

Right now, Lily was snuggled up under the quilt Caleb had tucked around her and staring at the fire Ethan had built in the fireplace. Allen had brought her some of the books she had set aside in the den she had been planning on reading. He sat at the end of the couch with her feet on his lap and picked up a book.

"Guess it's my turn to read to you," Allen said with a grin.

He was rubbing Lily's feet and she let out a contented sigh. She wanted to feel him rubbing her in other places. She slid one foot over his crotch, smiling when she felt his body jerk and his cock grow under it.

"Behave, Lily," Allen said huskily, his eyes growing darker with desire. "You need to rest and heal before we make love to you again."

Lily's lower lip poked out in a pout. "I want you, Allen."

"I want you too, honey," Allen said tenderly. "Soon."

The days passed quickly. The men always made sure at least one of them stayed with her. Helen came over almost daily, and she and Lily's friendship grew even deeper.

For the first time, Lily felt like she could be herself. Helen had confided she had read Lily's journal before she had given it to Ethan. She asked Lily questions, and Lily answered them as best she could.

A week after Lily came home, she and Helen decided to make Christmas cookies for all the ranch hands. Caleb was sitting at the table eating some of them. He said he was the official taste tester to make sure they were edible.

"Lily, can I ask you a question that has been bugging me?" Helen said as she placed more cookie dough on the cookie sheet.

"Sure," Lily said, reaching for the oven mitts.

"How old are you?" Helen inquired.

Lily paused as she took another batch of cookies out of the oven. Turning she looked under her eyelashes at Caleb. He had a cookie halfway to his mouth. His eyes jumped to Lily.

Lily blushed, trying to think of how to answer the question. "I'm almost eighteen if you go by the age I died." She looked nervously at Caleb before adding, "But if you calculate it from the year I was born I'm one hundred and nine."

"You were only seventeen when you died?" Caleb choked out, turning pale.

"I was a month away from my eighteenth birthday," Lily insisted. "Many of the girls who were my age had already married and had children. Why, James Butler asked for my hand when I was fifteen."

Caleb stood up and walked toward Lily menacingly. "You are only seventeen?" He seemed to stress each word.

Lily looked pleadingly at Helen, "No, not if you look at the year I was born. I might look seventeen, but I'm not technically. It really doesn't matter. I mean. If you really want to look at it, I'm older than all of you. Isn't that right, Helen?"

Helen choked back a laugh. "I think I'll go see if Clive would mind going with me to drop a batch of these cookies off."

"Traitor!" Lily called desperately at Helen's retreating back. Looking at Caleb, who looked like he was about to have a stroke from the color of his face, Lily reached out her hands beseechingly. "Caleb, it doesn't matter."

"Like hell it doesn't matter. Shit, Lily. You would be jailbait." Caleb ran his hands through his short hair, pacing back and forth. "Shit!"

Allen and Ethan were coming in the back door when they heard Caleb's loud expletive.

"What's wrong?" Allen asked, looking back and forth between Lily's pleading eyes and Caleb's pale face.

"Wrong? Wrong?" Caleb shouted. "I'll tell you what's fucking wrong. Lily's only seventeen. That's what's fucking wrong. What we did to her was what is fucking wrong."

Lily drew back as if Caleb had hit her. Tears welled up in her eyes and spilled over as she stared at him.

"You regret making love to me?" Lily asked in a strangled voice. Caleb just turned and stared at her silently.

"Do you regret making love to me?" she said louder, starting to get mad. She turned to the other two men staring at her in disbelief and horror. "Do you? Do you regret making love to me?

"Lily, you don't understand. What we did to you? The three of us..." Ethan said in a strangled voice. "I'm almost old enough to be your father," he said with a shudder.

Lily pulled back from them. She looked at Allen, who was having a hard time looking her in the eye. "Allen?" Lily called out softly. When he still refused to look at her, she pressed. "Allen. Do you regret making love to me?"

Allen cleared his throat and opened his mouth, but nothing came out. Lily looked at the three men with growing anger.

"Well, let me tell you this. I don't regret it. What you did to me was beautiful, and I want more. I need more. My body may be the body of a seventeen-year-old, but the rest of me isn't. I love you, all of you. I want to be with you. If you can't accept that, then figure out a way to get over it," Lily said hotly. She turned off the oven and glared at the men one more time before she grabbed her jacket and stormed out the back door.

"Shit," Ethan said as he leaned against the refrigerator. "I knew she was young, but not that young."

Allen looked at his brothers. "What are we going to do?"

Caleb and Ethan both shifted uncomfortably. Ethan was the one who replied, "I need a drink."

"I'm with you," Caleb said, standing and grabbing his hat.

Allen let out a defeated sigh. "Me, too."

Grabbing their jackets and hats the three men headed outside. Ethan started the truck. "Allen, go ask Ed to keep an eye on Lily. Tell him we'll be back in a few hours." Allen nodded and jogged over to the barn.

"Hey, Ed," Allen called. Ed came out of the little office they had built in the back of the barn.

"Yeah, boss man."

"Can you keep an eye on Lily for a little while? My brothers and I need to go to town," Allen said uneasily.

Ed studied Allen carefully before replying, "Sure thing, boss. Just make sure you think twice before you screw up. Lily's different. I'd sure hate to see her hurt."

Allen just nodded before turning and heading back to the truck. Ed stood watching as the taillights faded into the distance. When he turned around Lily was standing behind him. She stared at the retreating truck with tears in her eyes. Ed let out a deep sigh before putting his arm around her shoulders.

"Give them boys time. They'll come around. In the meantime, I have a present for you from Clive. Seems at least one little guy misses you," Ed said as he opened the door to the warm office. Walking in, Lily heard a small meow. Dropping to her knees, she picked up the little kitten and held him close to her.

"Oh, Edison." Lily held the kitten tight to her, scratching him behind his ears as he purred.

"Clive kept him in here. Figured it was safer than taking him home. He's got a big hound dog and didn't want to take a chance of your kitten getting hurt," Ed said as he went to sit down on the old couch. He had a small television on, tuned to the weather channel.

"Thank you, Ed." Lily sighed again as she stood up and went to sit in the old armchair. Placing the kitten on her lap, she watched the weather for a little while before speaking.

"Ed?" Lily asked softly. "Do you think I'm too young?"

Ed looked at Lily carefully before replying, "You're special, Lily. There's something different about you like I told Allen. You may be wrapped up in a young package, but your eyes... your eyes tell a different story. Kind of like you've lived for a long, long time," he paused a minute before turning back around. "No, girl. I don't think you are too young at all."

Lily stood up, holding the kitten tight against her. Moving to the couch, she leaned over and kissed Ed's withered cheek. "Thank you. I think I'll go up to the house and clean up. The kitchen is a mess."

Ed nodded. "Lock the doors. I'll be around and so will some of the other men, but I'd feel better if you had the doors locked." Lily murmured her agreement as she walked out.

The rest of the afternoon passed slowly. Lily had finished cleaning not only the kitchen, but the rest of the house. Just when she thought she would go nuts, she heard the sound of a truck outside. Hoping the men had come back early, in a better mood, she peeked out the front door to see Brad and Harold getting out of the truck and hopping up the front steps. Curious to see what was going on, Lily opened the door before they had a chance to knock.

"Hey, guys. What are you up to?" Lily asked as she pushed a stray strand away from her face.

"Kidnapping you!" Harold said. "Ouch! What did you do that for?"

"You dolt! Watch what you say," Brad growled. "Lily, we're taking some of the kids in town on a hay ride and wondered if you would like to go. They're going to be singing Christmas carols and drinking hot chocolate."

Lily's eyes lit up. "Oh yes, thank you. I'd love to go. I need to grab my jacket and some warmer boots. Oh, I need to tell Ed as well."

"I'll tell Ed. You get your stuff. We'll meet you outside," Brad said.

Lily rushed through the house, grabbing her heavy jacket and pulled on an extra pair of socks before shoving her feet into her boots. She was so excited. She hadn't been on a hay ride since she was little, and that was a very long time ago. Rushing out, she locked the door and practically jumped into Brad's waiting arms.

"Oh, thank you for thinking of me," Lily said breathlessly.

Brad stared down into Lily's flushed face and couldn't resist dropping a light kiss on her lips. "Anytime, Lily." Lily blushed and smiled.

"Come on you two, or we're going to be late," Harold said from the driver's seat. Lily climbed in the middle between the two men and buckled up. She giggled with excitement as they pulled away.

..*

"Pour me another one," Caleb growled, holding his glass out for another beer.

"So, what do we do? We've been sitting here for half the day and still haven't come to a decision," Allen said. He had switched to coffee an hour before, thinking at least one of them needed to be sober enough to drive home. He looked up when the door opened to the bar and Matt Holden walked in. Matt saw them and headed straight for their table, frowning.

"What are all three of you doing here?" he demanded, pulling out a chair and sitting down. "Why aren't one of you watching over Lily?"

Caleb scowled at Matt. "Do you know how old she is?" he slurred. "She's fucking jailbait."

Matt looked at Caleb before turning to stare at Ethan and Allen. He took a drink and waited a moment before asking, "How do you figure she's jailbait?"

Caleb glared at Matt and took another deep swig of his beer. Ethan sighed deeply before replying, "She's seventeen, Matt."

"Is she?" Matt asked calmly.

"You've seen her. What do you think?" Ethan demanded.

"Well, if she is the same Lily O'Donnell from all the reports I have—and she sure as hell looks like her—I'd figure she looks pretty damn good for her age," Matt said as he poured more beer into his glass.

"What do you mean she looks pretty damn good?" Caleb asked. "What are you doing looking at her? She's ours, goddam-m-mit. Keep your fucking eyes off her."

Matt laughed and held up his hands in surrender. "Calm down, Caleb. Damn. You asked me my opinion, and legally I'm giving it to you. If she is the same Lily O'Donnell who went missing all those years ago, and I'm not saying she is, then by my calculations she is well over the age of consent."

"How do you figure that?" Ethan asked.

"Legally you go by the date she was born. If she was born before nineteen ninety-four she is not jailbait," Matt said with a twinkle in his eye. "You do have to admit she does look good for her age, though."

"Damn," Allen said as he sat for a moment. "He's right."

Caleb leaned forward, slamming his hands down on the table, "Well, why the hell didn't we think of that earlier?"

"Lily did," Ethan replied. "She tried telling us in the kitchen, only we weren't listening. We couldn't see beyond her outer appearance."

Caleb stood unsteadily. "Well, shit a brick. Let's go home, then."

Matt stood up and grabbed Caleb by the arm and forced him to sit back down. "I think you need to sober up a little first before you head home. I don't think Lily would be happy to see you drunk. Lynn, bring a pot of coffee."

Chapter 14

"What the fuck do you mean she's not here?" Allen roared at Ed.

It had taken almost another two hours to sober Caleb and Ethan up enough to drive home. Matt had talked about the leads they were following from the camping gear they had found at the old homestead. It looked like a man by the name of Peter Canton had purchased the items in Jackson a month and a half before. They had traced him through his credit card. So far, though, they hadn't had any luck in locating him. They also couldn't figure out why he was after Lily.

All three of them had been quiet on the drive home. When they had pulled up and discovered the house dark and silent, they had panicked until Ed had come out of the office in the barn to let them know Brad and Harold had taken off with Lily several hours ago.

"Where the fuck did they take her? I called the bunkhouse, and the men there didn't know. I've called Brad and Harold's cell phones and didn't get an answer either," Allen said frustrated.

It was almost two hours later before they heard a truck coming down the drive. Ethan looked out the window. The men had gotten cleaned up, were totally sober, and madder than hell. They had called Brad and Harold's cell phones again and again without getting an answer. They were to the point they were going to call Matt and have him call out a search party.

Ethan looked over his shoulder as Caleb and Allen came to watch as the truck pulled up. The light in the cab came on, and they watched with growing anger as Lily laughed and gave Harold a kiss on his cheek before sliding out of the cab and right into Brad's arms. Allen and Caleb both took off for the door when they saw Brad lean down and gently kiss Lily on the lips.

"Aw, fuck," Ethan said quietly. He could feel his blood beginning to boil.

Allen and Caleb fought over the door trying to get it opened. It slammed back against the wall as Caleb finally wrenched it from Allen's hand. Both men were standing on the porch with clenched fists, watching as Brad led Lily up to it.

"Where the fuck have you been? We've been calling you for the past two hours," Allen said through clenched teeth.

"Allen, your language," Lily admonished. "Brad and Harold took me on a hay ride, and I had a wonderful time. Not that it is any of your business," she added as she came up to them. Turning, she smiled at Brad again. "Thank you again for a wonderful evening."

"Our pleasure, Lily. Night," Brad said with a smirk at Allen and Caleb. "See you tomorrow."

Allen and Caleb glared at Brad before turning to follow Lily into the house. She took off her jacket and gloves, hanging them on the hat rack to dry before taking off her boots and setting them aside. Ethan stood in the living room with his arms folded across his chest.

"Just how much pleasure did you give them, Lily?" Caleb asked darkly.

Lily turned narrowed eyes on Caleb, before shrugging her shoulders, "I really don't think it is any of your concern. I'm tired. I think I'll turn in for the night," she said as she started to move toward the kitchen.

"Lily, Caleb asked you a question. I would like to know the answer to it as well," Ethan said quietly.

Lily turned and looked at all three men. "You made your feelings perfectly clear when you took off this morning leaving me alone. Obviously you don't care about me the way I thought you did. So as far as I'm concerned, what I do in my spare time is none of your business!" she finished hotly.

She had no idea how beautiful she looked standing there with her eyes flashing and her face flushed. Turning to go into the kitchen, she let out a squeal when Allen grabbed her from behind. He swung her around and kissed her deeply.

"Don't tell me I don't care about you. You are ours, Lily," Allen said. "Now, answer Caleb, baby, because we are fixing to show you just how much you are ours."

Lily's breath caught in her throat as she stared up into Allen's dark eyes. "They just took me on a hay ride with the kids in town. We sang Christmas carols and drank hot chocolate. They were perfect gentlemen."

Allen slid his hand down Lily's back to cup her ass, pulling her against him. "Tonight is my turn,

Lily. I want you, baby. I want to fuck your beautiful ass," Allen whispered against her ear as he pressed her tightly against him. "All three of us are going to take you at the same time, baby. We're going to show you just how much we love you and want you."

Lily shivered as she felt Caleb and Ethan come up behind her. Caleb tilted her head back and kissed her before Ethan turned her face to his. Lily was on fire. Allen nodded to Ethan before he pulled away.

"Lily, go up to the master bedroom and get in the shower. Ethan is going to help you. Caleb and I'll be up shortly."

Lily gasped as Ethan picked her up and started walking toward the staircase. She trembled as she looked over Ethan's shoulder and into Allen's and Caleb's eyes. They held a promise she had only dreamed about. Burying her face in Ethan's neck, she couldn't suppress the growing moisture between her legs.

Ethan carried Lily into the master bathroom and set her down gently. Moving back, he folded his arms across his chest.

"Strip," he said harshly.

Lily's head jerked up to stare at Ethan. She could tell he was still angry. "Ethan?" she asked uncertainly.

"Strip, Lily. I want to see you naked," Ethan ordered tightly.

Lily nodded as she unbuttoned her blouse. She let it slide down her arms where it fell to the floor at her feet. Next, she undid the buttons of her jeans, pushing them until they rested around her feet. She had taken her boots off inside the door so all she had on were her socks. She used the toe of each foot to help pull them off and stepped out of them until she was standing in just her bra and panties.

Ethan sucked in a breath. "Damn, Lily. You are so beautiful."

Lily laughed softly. "You know, between you, Allen, and Caleb all my cursing jars are going to be overflowing."

Ethan just grinned at her wickedly. "Take off your bra and panties. I want you in the shower. We're going to watch you as you shower."

Lily's body flushed with desire. They wanted to watch her shower, did they? Well, she would show them just how good a shower could be. Turning her back to him, she looked over her shoulder as she unhooked the front clasp on her bra and let it fall away. Hooking her fingers in the waistband of her panties, she slid them slowly down her hips, wiggling her ass just enough to get them to fall the rest of the way. She smiled to herself when she heard Ethan's breathing getting heavier.

"Shit," Caleb said from the doorway.

Lily looked over her shoulder as she stepped into the shower to see Allen and Caleb standing behind Ethan. Lily slid the clear glass door shut behind her and turned on first one, then the other shower head so the water fell like rain over her. She undid her braid and ran her fingers through her hair so it flowed down her back.

Raising her arms above her head, she closed her eyes and tilted her face back, letting the water pour over her in glistening trails, turning to give the men a side view of her full breasts and flat stomach. The water felt like it was making love to her skin as it ran in rivets over her beaded nipples, drops hanging from them before running further down.

She reached over and pick up the bar of soap and a washcloth. She began lathering herself, running her hands over her arms, up her flat stomach to cup her breasts, then letting her hands slide down between her legs. She was so hot she was already swollen with need. She moaned as she ran her soapy hands over her swollen mound, wishing it was one of her men washing her.

Allen couldn't stand it any longer. He had already unbuttoned his shirt and pulled it off by the time the water started. When Lily had turned sideways it was too much. He was pulling his pants off and heading for the shower by the time she had the soap in her hand.

Ethan and Caleb nodded at him and headed for the bedroom. They had a special punishment for Lily waiting. She needed to learn she was theirs. Lily moaned when she felt Allen's calloused hands rub over the soft skin of her hips. She started to lean back against him, but he took her arms and placed them against the wall of the shower.

"Stay like that," he whispered.

Lily let her head drop forward as she felt him take the washcloth out of her hand. He slowly began washing her. She bit back a moan as his hands slid over her breasts, rubbing the soft cloth over her engorged nipples.

Biting her lip, it took every ounce of willpower not to turn in his arms and press herself against him. His hands slid further down between her legs. Pushing on them until they spread wide open for him, he washed her, taking his time before moving down her leg. He gently picked up one foot and washed it before rinsing it and setting it down and doing the same to the other foot.

Lily shivered when she felt him press a kiss to the inside of her ankle. He was killing her one slow stroke at a time. No longer able to hold back the moans, she wiggled as he moved further up her leg.

"Lean farther back and spread your legs wider for me," Allen said softly against her ear.

Lily leaned even further back and spread her legs. She gasped as Allen ran the washcloth between the cheeks of her ass, stroking her tight ring with his finger.

"This is mine. I watched as Caleb took your virgin pussy, and it turned me on. I watched while Ethan took your virgin mouth, and it turned me on even more. Tonight, they are going to watch while I take your virgin ass, Lily. Tonight you are going to belong to all three of us."

Lily panted at the image Allen was painting. To belong to all three of them totally, unconditionally was more than she could ever hope for. Allen reached over and turned off the water. Opening the door to the shower, he grabbed a large towel and wrapped it around her.

"Go into the bedroom," Allen directed. Lily looked at Allen before reaching up to pull his head down to hers. She kissed him deeply before she felt the sharp smack on her ass. "Go now before I take you right here."

Lily smiled seductively before walking to the door. She stood in the doorway to the bedroom, unsure of what to do. The covers on the bed were turned down and the only lighting in the room came from a small lamp next to the bed and the glow from the fireplace.

She glanced at Ethan, who motioned for her to come stand in front of him. Both he and Caleb were undressed except for their boxers. Lily walked over until she stood in front of Ethan.

He gently tugged on the towel until she let it go. Caleb had another towel and was drying her long hair. Caleb threw the towel onto the bed and picked up a comb and began combing her hair, using slow strokes as if he were making love to it. The gentle tugs combined with Ethan rubbing the towel over her body had Lily reaching out to touch them.

"Oh no, baby. You don't get to touch. Not yet anyway," Caleb growled, giving a sharp tug to her hair as he braided it.

"Why? I want to touch you so much. Why, Caleb?" Lily moaned.

"You were a bad girl tonight," Ethan said, sliding the towel between Lily's legs. She couldn't resist rubbing her swollen mound against the towel and Ethan's hand.

A sharp slap to her ass made her jump. "Not yet, Lily," Allen said.

"But why? Why do you think I was bad?" Lily asked, shivering with need. The slap to her ass had made her even hotter than before. "What did I do?"

Allen looked at Ethan. "Ethan, get on the bed. I want to see her suck on you."

Ethan walked over to the bed pulling off his boxers as he went. Tossing them to one side, he climbed on the bed and lay back against the headboard, spreading his legs.

"Come here, Lily," Ethan demanded.

Lily couldn't help licking her lips as she walked toward the end of the bed. Climbing up, she crawled toward Ethan slowly on her hands and knees, giving Caleb and Allen a view of her lush ass and moist pussy.

"Damn, she's got a beautiful ass. I can't wait to watch you fuck it," Caleb said with a moan.

"Get the clamps, Caleb. I have a feeling this is going to be sheer torture for all of us," Allen said tightly.

Lily was totally focused on the beautiful view in front of her. Ethan was thick and long, and she loved the taste of him. She wondered vaguely how he would feel inside of her.

They had only made love once before and Ethan had not taken her that way yet. She desperately wanted to feel him buried deep inside her. She knew he would stretch her, but she burned for him.

Licking her lips again, she ran her tongue over the tip of Ethan's broad head, tasting the pre-cum beaded on the end. Moaning, she slid him into her mouth as far as she could take him before pulling him almost all the way out of her mouth.

Ethan jumped. He hadn't expected her to clamp down on him so fast, and it took him by surprise. Groaning, he buried his hands in her hair while pushing up with his hips.

"Goddammit. She's hot."

"Hold her still while Caleb gets her nipples ready. We need her burning for us tonight when we all take her," Allen said, unable to take his eyes off the beautiful sight of Lily giving his brother head.

Caleb sat down on the bed next to Lily and pinched her nipple between his fingers, rolling it back and forth until it swelled and peaked. "Shit, Ethan. It is so sexy watching her eat you," Caleb said as he reached under and clamped a nipple clamp onto one of Lily's nipples.

Lily jumped when she felt the clamp tighten around her nipple. When Caleb did it to her other nipple the feelings they aroused in her were too much, and she moaned around Ethan's cock, the vibrations running down the length of it.

"You guys better hurry the hell up. She likes this, and at the rate she's stroking me I'm not sure I'll last," Ethan said, breathless.

He could feel his balls beginning to tighten up. He fought the feelings building inside him wanting to make it last as long as possible. They had plans, and he didn't want to ruin them.

Caleb pulled a chain between the clamps to connect the two together, then handed it to Ethan. "Pull on them."

Allen came up behind Lily and ran his fingers between the folds of her moist mound. He slid a finger in slowly. Lily clamped down on the finger sliding into her pussy with a cry, pulling away from Ethan's cock as she felt him go deeper.

"I think she likes that too," Ethan said with a smile. "You like being fucked, don't you?"

Lily couldn't answer. Her whole body was on overload. She wanted relief from the pressure building up inside her.

Panting, she nodded her head. "More."

Caleb ran his hand down along the curve of Lily's back and ass before sliding his finger into her pussy.

"Did you ever feel anything so hot, Allen?" Caleb asked as he began pumping his finger in and out of her pussy at the same time Allen did.

Lily started sobbing. "Please. Oh, please."

Allen smacked Lily's ass. "Please what, darling?"

"It's too much," Lily cried out as she pushed her ass higher. The smack hadn't hurt. If anything, it had turned her even hotter.

"No, it's not, baby. Soon, soon you'll know what it's like to have too much," Allen said as he stroked Lily's ass, rubbing his finger up from her wet pussy to slide it around her tight ring. "Caleb, get me the lube. Ethan, I think Lily should feel just how full you can make her," Allen continued as he took the lube from Caleb.

Ethan gently leaned Lily up enough for him to slide down the bed. "Come on, baby. Straddle me."

Lily shuddered as the weight of the clamps pulled her nipples when she moved. She opened her legs, allowing enough room for Ethan to slide between her legs. As she felt his long length push against her sensitive mound, she whimpered.

"Grab me, Lily, and guide me into your pussy," Ethan demanded huskily.

Lily had her hands braced on his shoulders and was leaning forward. Ethan could grab the chain between her breasts with his teeth if he wanted to and pull her further down. He was tempted, but he didn't know if he would be able to last if she clamped down on his cock yet.

He felt Lily grab his hard length and guide it to the opening of her wet pussy. He pushed up with his hips at the same time he pulled her down by hers. Both of them groaned loudly when she was fully seated on his cock. Lily put her hands back down on his shoulders and began to use her knees to ride him.

"Shit a gold brick, but she is so damn tight," Ethan choked out. "You better fucking do what you want to do because I'm not going to last."

Allen pushed Lily forward until her hands rested on either side of Ethan's head and her lips were inches from his. "Lily, relax for me as much as you can. I need to stretch you before I take you. Okay, baby?"

His hands were trembling as he poured lube onto his fingers. Spreading the cheeks of her ass, he rubbed some lube on her tight ring before he slid his finger through it.

Lily gasped at the burning sensation, but it quickly turned to heat. Caleb moved to watch as Allen slid another finger into Lily's tight ass. He rubbed her back and hip as he watched. When Allen slid three fingers into her tight ring, Ethan's expletive filled the air.

"Shit, she is clamping down on me hard again."

"Relax, baby," Caleb said, rubbing her. "You are so beautiful."

"Oh, Caleb," Lily whimpered.

Allen nodded to Caleb, who moved to kneel beside Lily. Allen braced his legs and moved his cock behind Lily, pressing the head into her tight ring.

"You belong to us, Lily. For always," he said as he slowly pushed into her.

Lily groaned as the burning increased. Just when she thought she couldn't take any more, Allen pushed through the tight ring and slid deep into her ass. Sweat beaded on his forehead as he gave her time to adjust to him.

"Oh, Allen," Lily said, trying to move back against him.

"Wait, Lily. I don't want to hurt you," Allen said through clenched teeth. He moved slowly, pulling out a little ways, then pushing back in.

Lily shook from the fullness. Never had she expected to feel like this. To feel so loved and needed. Ethan groaned as he felt her move, trying to push down and back at the same time.

"Let us do the moving, baby. You just feel," Ethan said as he began a rhythm of pushing in while Allen pulled out.

Caleb gently pulled Lily's head up until her mouth was aligned with his cock. "Open your mouth, Lily. Take us all in."

Lily obeyed, unable to do anything else. She was operating on feelings alone and no longer in control of her body. As Caleb slid his hard cock into her mouth, she moaned again.

Caleb pulled gently on the chain between her breasts, tugging on her nipples. The sensation was too much for her overloaded body, and Lily climaxed. Her vaginal walls clamped down hard on Ethan, and he cried out as he came hard and deep inside her, pumping his seed deep.

Allen was unable to contain himself any longer. He had been on fire in the shower, and it had taken every bit of his willpower not to come when he had finally been seated in Lily's tight ass. The feel of her clamping down on his brother's cock was more than he could handle, and he emptied himself, draping himself across Lily's back and gripping her hips as he did.

Caleb's expletive followed shortly afterward as Lily's moans and sucking mouth clamped down on him. With a shudder, he came deep in her throat, holding her hair tightly in his hand to prevent her from pulling away. It was only after she had swallowed the last drop that he released her.

Lily was completely shattered. The climax had been so intense her body still rocked from the aftershocks of it. She cried out as Allen pulled out of her, and she collapsed on top of Ethan's broad chest, unable to move. Sobs shook her body as she tried to piece her shattered mind back together.

Ethan held Lily tightly as she tried to draw in a shuddering breath, her sobs echoing throughout the room.

Caleb leaned down next to her. "Lily, baby. Are you hurt? Did we hurt you?"

Allen looked anxiously at Ethan and Caleb. Lily couldn't speak, so she just shook her head. No, they had not hurt her. They had given her the most wonderful experience of her life. She had never felt so loved, so needed, so wanted. How could she ever communicate to them how much she loved them? How much she needed them?

Allen went into the bathroom and came out with a warm washcloth. He gently cleaned Lily. Throwing the washcloth down onto one of the towels, he climbed onto the bed and pulled the covers up before drawing Lily into his arms.

Ethan rolled out from under Lily and got up. He went into the bathroom to clean up and took the dirty towels with him. When he came back out he stared down at Lily's closed eyes. He felt so much love for her he felt like he would explode. Shaken by the overwhelming feelings he looked at his brothers and saw they felt the same way.

"Stay with her. I have some things to do. I want to review what Matt told us earlier. I don't want that bastard to ever get his hands on her again." Caleb had climbed in on the other side of Lily and was running his hand over her face. Both he and Allen nodded silently.

Chapter 15

As Christmas drew closer, Lily glowed from the love the men were giving her. One of them always stayed with her. Each morning she woke wrapped in the arms of one of them. Sometimes during the day the one who had stayed with her would sneak up behind her, and they would end up making love.

One day Ethan had called Lily into his office and had taken her right there on his desk. She had been flushed and achy the rest of the day. Another time she had been in the basement sorting clothes when Allen had come downstairs. He had tied her up and taken her as she clung to him with her hands tied above her head and her legs locked around his waist.

Caleb had taken her in the shower this morning. She blushed as she remembered some of the things he had done to her. She had been well and thoroughly loved. By the time he had gotten done with her, she had slept another hour.

The nights were still for all of them. Some nights they made passionate love; other nights they would sit curled up downstairs in the living room talking, watching television, or quietly reading. Lily felt their love flowing through her and couldn't believe she had been so blessed. She had been at the ranch for almost three months. Christmas was fast approaching and with it came a sense that her time was drawing to a close.

She felt a tear track down her cheek. She wiped it away angrily. She wouldn't go this time. She wanted to stay. This was where she belonged. Lily looked up as the door opened. She smiled when she saw Ethan and Allen walk in the kitchen.

"You're home early," she said, walking over to give them both a kiss.

"We thought you might like to go into town today to do some Christmas shopping. Ethan needs to talk to Matt and Caleb, and I have some free time. We thought we could grab dinner at the diner and save you from having to cook tonight," Allen said as he wrapped his cold hands around her waist.

Squealing as the cold hands touched her stomach. Lily turned in his arms and put hers around his neck. "Oh, that sounds like a wonderful idea. I haven't been to town since the hay ride."

Both men frowned. They didn't like remembering seeing her with Brad and his lips on hers. Lily ran her fingers over Allen's forehead leaning forward she whispered. "Just remember what happened afterward."

Allen's frown cleared immediately, and he groaned. "Maybe we can have a repeat performance before we go."

Lily just laughed and pulled away. "If we do, I won't be going anywhere. You guys short-circuit me every time you love me like that, and I can't move for hours afterward."

Ethan sighed. "Well, I guess if we take you shopping first, then we can come home and love you."

Caleb walked into the room as Ethan was finishing his suggestion. "Sounds good to me." Lily flashed him a look of disbelief remembering what they had done just a few hours before. Flushing, she realized she was getting wet thinking about it.

Lily was excited about the shopping, Christmas was just a couple of days away, and she wanted to pick up a few things. She practically danced from one shop to another with Allen and Caleb alternating between laughing and groaning as the packages began to accumulate.

Lily looped her hands around each of their arms as they walked across the street to the diner. They were meeting Ethan there. Lily smiled at Gladys and her husbands as she slid into the booth next to Ethan. She gave him a warm kiss and snuggled up to him.

"I missed you today," she said shyly.

"So did we," Allen joked. "We could have used some help emptying the stores. I think Lily bought them out."

Lily pouted over at Allen. "I did not."

Ethan sat back, smiling as he watched the teasing going back and forth between his brothers and Lily. They had changed so much since she had come into their lives. He laid his arm along the back of the booth, playing with Lily's hair as she turned outraged eyes to Gladys.

"Do you hear these two? You'd think I tortured them all day long." Gladys laughed as Allen and Caleb tried to defend themselves.

"You boys might as well give up," Earl called out. "You'll never win this argument." Carl laughed behind the counter.

They placed their order and enjoyed the meal surrounded by good friends, unaware they were being observed. Peter Canton lowered the binoculars. He shivered in the cold. He sat in an old pickup truck parked across the street. He had been watching the girl and the two men with her all day.

He had been having to move frequently and was almost out of cash. He couldn't use his credit cards any longer for fear of being tracked. He had cursed under his breath when he realized he had paid for the stuff left at the old house with one.

Now, he didn't trust using one in case they could find him. He had to get the O'Donnell girl soon. He couldn't keep sleeping out of doors like he had been. He was freezing his ass off. He had hoped they would have dropped their guard by now, but the bitch was never alone. It seemed one of those bastards was always with her.

He had noticed, though, that it was always just one, not all three. He had been watching the house every day for the past two weeks hiding in the woods. Once he had even been able to get into the barn and had hidden in the loft.

He figured if he could get it down to just two of them, he could kill the man and take the girl. If she didn't come quietly, he would get the information out of her and kill her too. Not that she would stay dead for long, but it would give him time to get away, and he could disappear again.

Once he was immortal, he could take his time gathering wealth. He would have forever, and he could live like a king. Pulling his hat further down over his face, he acted like he was looking for something before he turned on the truck and pulled away. After Christmas he would take her out. He planned on being immortal by the first of the year.

Christmas morning dawned with the sky's heavy with snow. It would be a quiet day for everyone. Most of the ranch hands had left for a couple of days reprieve with just the bare minimum staying to care for the livestock. Ed was going over to Clive and Helen's for Christmas dinner. Their kids and grandkids were in for the holiday, and Helen had a houseful. She had asked Lily if they wanted to come over, but Lily had felt selfish—she wanted to spend Christmas in her home with her men.

She had gotten up early, sliding out between the warm bodies of Ethan and Caleb. Allen had slept in his room last night. They seemed to take turns who would sleep with her. Sometimes she would go to sleep with one brother only to wake up in the arms of another.

She glanced at them and smiled. Her life was so full. Turning, she walked silently out of the bedroom and down the stairs. The Christmas tree lit up the room when she turned it on. Sinking down on her knees, she bowed her head in silent prayer.

Please, if you can hear this, please let me stay this time. I love them so much. Momma and Da, if you can hear me, I just want to let you know I'm doing well. I've finally found what it means to have a love like yours. I wish you could meet them. Ethan, Caleb, and Allen have brought me so much happiness and love. Mrs. Cunnings, if you and the dads are listening, thank you for having such wonderful boys to let me share my life and love with. I miss you, Momma and Da. I'll always be your faithful daughter. Merry Christmas.

Allen stood on the bottom step of the stairs watching as Lily knelt and bowed her head. He had never seen anyone so beautiful in all his life. He loved her so much it hurt sometimes. He knew Lily still feared her time with them was going to be short and deep down he was terrified she might be right.

They had had Doc Harley check her out while she had been in the hospital, and he said except for the injuries she had received during her abduction everything came back normal. They had all gone ahead and had blood tests done. Today was a special day for them. He, Ethan, and Caleb were going to ask Lily to marry them. They had picked out a ring, and Ethan had picked it up the day they had gone into town.

They knew there was a good chance Lily could be pregnant. None of them had used any type of protection when they had made love to her, which was almost daily. Lily never asked about it, and she had told Doc Harley she wasn't taking any medications including birth control.

Allen closed his eyes as a sharp emotion stabbed at him when he thought of Lily big and round with their child. They didn't care who the father was—they would all be a dad. He knew Lily would be even more beautiful as she got bigger. The thought of her big and blooming turned him on. He felt his cock throb at the thought of being buried deep inside her.

"Lily," Allen said quietly.

Lily gasped when she heard Allen call her name. She still couldn't get used to how quietly he could move sometimes. Staring up at him, she saw the evidence of his desire for her in his eyes and his body.

He didn't try to hide the huge hard-on he had tenting the front of his pajama bottoms.

Lily let her eyes roam over his bare chest. She felt a matching desire burn inside her. Lifting her hand to him, Lily beckoned him to her silently. Allen walked over, pulling her gently up and into his arms.

Not saying a word he took her over to the thick rug in front of the fireplace. Bending, he began untying the ribbons, holding her robe and letting it drop to the floor. He ran light kisses along her jaw as he slipped first one, then the other strap of her nightgown off her shoulders, so it too puddled on the floor around her, leaving her bare in the warm glow of the fireplace.

Lily shivered as she felt Allen's hot breath over one of her breasts. The feel of him sucking on her raced through her body, causing her pussy to clench in desperate desire. Groaning, she wrapped her arms around his head, arching her breasts toward him for more.

Allen pulled back to look at Lily's upturned face. He pulled her down, laying her gently on the rug. Still looking at her, he pushed her thighs apart and lowered his mouth to her hot mound. Lily cried out and clenched the rug with both fists as his hot mouth closed over her clit.

Allen sucked and pulled on her swollen nub, tasting the sweet nectar of her feminine juices. He slid his tongue in and out of her, then lapped her like a kitten lapping milk. Lily began shaking as she felt him loving her. Panting, she tried to hold back the climax she felt building, but she couldn't. Screaming out, she came hard, pressing herself down against Allen's hot mouth.

"Shit, if that isn't the best Christmas present I've ever seen," Caleb said from the stairs.

Ethan looked down on Lily spread out like an offering in front of the fire. Her hair was spread out around her face, framing it. Her arms were out to her sides where she gripped the thick rug, and her knees were bent and spread in offering to Allen's mouth.

Allen looked up and grinned. "I wondered when you two were going to get your asses down here. I couldn't wait any longer to wish Lily a Merry Christmas."

Ethan looked at Lily and smiled darkly. "I drew the short straw last night, Lily. Today is about my fantasy."

Lily's nipples pebbled at the thought. She knew she was about to be well and truly loved by her men. Lying like an offering before them, all Lily could do was watch as Ethan and Caleb moved slowly down the stairs toward her. She licked her lips nervously. All three of them looked impressively hard. Ethan pushed his boxers down his legs. Caleb followed. Allen just grinned as he watched Lily's nervous response.

"Lily, take off Allen's pants and spread for him again. He has a surprise for you," Ethan said as he walked over to pick up a present from under the tree. Lily watched him as he handed the present to Allen. "This is for you, bro."

Allen stood so Lily could pull his pants off him. Lily looked at the other two men before turning back to Allen.

Allen took the gift with a wicked gleam in his eye. "Thanks, bro." He waited as Lily slowly sat up and got to her knees so she could pull Allen's pants off him. Grabbing the elastic waist, she pulled slowly, watching as his hard cock came free. Allen's cock was level with Lily's mouth, and she couldn't resist taking a swipe at it with her tongue. Allen jerked and groaned.

"You are a very bad girl, Lily. I think you need to be taught a lesson," Caleb said, watching as Lily's eyes darted to him before turning back to Allen's cock.

"If I'm going to be taught a lesson I might as well be very, very bad, then," Lily said quietly before she opened her mouth wide and took Allen's whole length into her mouth.

"Holy shit," Allen cursed. He jerked as Lily's mouth clamped down on his cock.

Caleb *tsk*ed as Ethan looked on wickedly. "Yes, she is being very, very naughty. I guess we'll just have to see what Santa put under the tree for her," Ethan said smugly.

"Lay her down, Allen," Caleb said. "I'll get you the stuff you'll need." He headed for the downstairs bathroom.

When he came back he had a towel, a washcloth, and a small container of warm water. He had Lily raise up so he could lay the towel under her. Lily bit her lip nervously as she watched silently.

Allen slowly opened his present to discover a razor. "Now what do you suppose this is for?" He said with a grin. Looking at Lily, then the razor again, he nodded to his brothers. "What do you think?"

"What?" Lily asked nervously. She stared suspiciously at the razor in Allen's hand, her eyes growing wide when she saw them looking at her dark mound. "Oh, no. Oh, no." Just the idea had her pussy getting wetter.

"Oh, yes," came three responses.

"Spread your legs wide for me, baby," Allen said softly. Lily closed her eyes and spread her legs, shivering as she felt Allen gently wash her, then the foam of the shaving cream before she felt the gentle swipe of the blade across her mound. Allen grinned as he felt her mound clench and wet pussy juice dripped down between her thighs. "She likes this. Merry Christmas, baby."

Lily groaned as she felt him clean her bare mound. It was so sensitive she cried out when he ran his fingers over her.

"Damn. If she liked this present, what do you think she'll think of some of the others?" Allen asked in awe. He couldn't resist bending over and rubbing his mouth over the bare mound.

Lily jerked upright, crying out, "Oh God, that feels so good."

Ethan and Caleb stared at her pale mound. Crouching down on either side of her, Ethan and Caleb each pushed a finger into her pussy. "Oh, hell yeah, she likes it. Caleb, I think you have a present or two under the tree."

Caleb grinned as he pulled his finger out of Lily's pussy and licked it, looking at her wickedly. "Let's see what Santa brought me to help teach you some manners."

He came back a moment later with a small box. Opening it, he pulled out a new set of nipple clamps. This was different from the other set he had used on her, though.

Lily frowned as she noticed three clamps instead of two. Why would there be three, she wondered. Not having a chance to ask, she was gently pushed back, and Ethan and Allen each took one of her wrists in their big hands and pulled her wide while Caleb moved between her legs forcing her to open up for him.

She moaned loudly when he clipped first one nipple, then the other. It was only when he reached down between her legs and pushed back her soft folds that she realized where the third clamp was going to go. Unable to contain the gasp as he gently tightened it, she groaned, trying to break the hold Ethan and Allen held on her arms.

"Oh, God, that feels so good. I'm on fire," she moaned as she wiggled. Each time she moved she felt the tug on her nipples.

"Wait until I connect them. It gets even better," Caleb said huskily.

He was on fire himself. Seeing her lying there letting them do to her what they wanted was such a turn-on. He had always liked to have a little of the edge when he made love, but he had no idea his brothers shared his desire. The fact they did, and that Lily was an eager student, made their relationship even more special. He pulled the chain out of the box and connected the two nipple clamps together before running it down to the one on her clit. When he tugged gently on it, Lily screamed as she came again.

"Shit, listen to her," Caleb said in awe. "I wonder if she is going to like your present as well, Ethan."

Ethan went over to the Christmas tree and pulled a slightly larger box out from under it. Lily panted as she watched Ethan come back to stand between her legs. He slowly unwrapped it to reveal a padded paddle. He whistled as he turned it around.

"Nice."

Lily's eyes grew large as she looked at the padded paddle. Her eyes darted from one of the men to the other. "Wait a minute. What are you going to do with that?"

"You have been a very, very naughty girl. All naughty girls need a good paddling every once in a while to keep them in line," Ethan said with a mischievous grin. "Up and on your hands and knees, Lily."

Lily shook her head. "No."

Caleb raised an eyebrow at Lily. "Did you just say 'no'?"

Allen ran his hands down her arm smiling. "You shouldn't tell any of us 'no,' baby. But, you definitely shouldn't tell Ethan 'no.'"

Lily looked back and forth before she slowly turned over onto her stomach. She gasped as the movement pulled on the clamps tugging on both her breasts and her clit. She got up on her hands and knees. Looking over her shoulder at Ethan, she was unable to resist wiggling her ass at him.

Ethan grinned. Turning the paddle over in his hand, he smacked Lily on the ass just enough to smart but not hurt her. Lily groaned as the impact of the paddle caused her pussy to clench. Ethan paddled her bottom until it was a soft pink. He tested her by sliding a finger into her pussy between hits. She was so wet her juices ran down the inside of her thigh. He swatted her one more time, and when she groaned loudly he knew he couldn't handle any more.

"I want her to straddle me," Ethan choked out.

Both his brothers looked as strained as he felt. Pulling Lily up, Allen and Caleb helped her position herself over Ethan. When she sank down, she impaled herself on his hard, straining cock. Ethan clenched her hips as she settled all the way down in one stroke. Lily looked at Ethan's face as she impaled herself. Ethan had thrown back his head and his mouth was slightly open as if he was in intense pleasure/pain.

Allen watched as Lily impaled herself on his brother. Turned on beyond anything he had ever experienced before, he grabbed the chains on the clamps and pulled Lily forward. When she opened her mouth to gasp at the sudden tension, he slid his cock into her mouth, burying it as far as he could without hurting her.

Lily sucked Allen, teasing him with her tongue and teeth. When he went to pull out, she let her teeth lightly scrape the length, and when he pushed deep, she let her tongue wrap around him. Allen shuddered at the combination of soft and sharp.

Caleb came up behind Lily. He watched as she gently rose up and slammed down on Ethan's cock. Grabbing her by the back of her neck, Caleb bent her forward and guided his cock to her tight ring. Ever since he had watched Allen fucking her there he knew he had to have a turn. She was so wet he didn't need lube. Sliding slowly into her, he groaned when she pushed back against him, taking him deeper. He lost what little control he had and began pumping her hard and fast. When she slammed down hard on Ethan, he roared out his release and gripped her hips to keep her still while Caleb pumped furiously in her ass. Ethan could feel every move his brother made through the thin barrier, and it was too much. He shuddered as he pressed her down hard against him, pumping his hot seed into her womb. He hoped he was successful in giving her a child. He wanted to see her growing big.

Caleb strained. He had felt Ethan's release and increased his strokes, the sounds of his flesh hitting Lily echoing throughout the room. His heavy panting matched Lily's and Ethan's. As he came, he pushed deeper, releasing his seed into Lily's body at the same time he felt her cries as she came. When she came, he felt her body spasm around his cock.

"Shit. Shit," Caleb and Ethan both said as their eyes widened in surprise to feel Lily milk a little more out of them.

Allen's loud cry filled the room a moment later as he jerked and threw his head back in release as Lily swallowed his hot cum. He fell back on his heels and bowed his head as he panted. He didn't know what had just happened, but it had been the most incredible experience of his life. He had always held a part of himself back, but he hadn't been able to this time. It was as if Lily had pulled his soul out of his body and into hers. It shook him to the very core of his being. He looked down at Lily's flushed face and knew he would never be the same. He would never be able to live without her. She had taken a piece of him. She had taken his heart.

Caleb was the one to gently pick Lily up and carry her upstairs to the master bathroom where he gently bathed her and dressed her. When he was done, he carried her back downstairs despite her insistence she could walk. He didn't want to let her go. He couldn't let her go. He needed to touch her. His brothers seemed to understand something had changed inside him. He had always been the one who could walk away. He was the one who always had a wall between him and the world. They seemed to sense his vulnerability. They seemed to understand he was in unfamiliar territory and needed Lily's reassurance everything would be all right.

Ethan fixed them a light breakfast and brought it into the living room to eat in front of the fire. Christmas music played softly in the background. When Lily had looked out the big windows she saw it had started to snow. She laughed as she listened to the men tell stories of Christmases past.

She handed out the presents she had made for each of the men. She didn't have much money and didn't want to spend theirs, so she had made things the way they did when she was a child. She shared some of the Christmases she had shared with her parents, crying a little as she remembered. Caleb had held her close while Ethan and Allen had scooted closer.

Finally, there was just one present left under the tree. It was a small box with Lily's name on it. Allen handed it to Caleb. They had decided they would flip to see who would be the one to legally marry Lily. Caleb had won the toss. It didn't matter to any of them who had won, because to them, she would be married to all three of them.

Caleb took the box from Allen, looking down at it a moment before he handed it to Lily. "This is for you from all of us."

Lily looked at Caleb, then down at the box she held. She slowly opened it. It was a small jeweler's box. Opening it, she saw a beautiful sapphire and diamond ring. Drawing in a breath, she raised tear-filled eyes to Caleb's again.

Caleb reached over and gently picked up Lily's hand, "Lily, will you marry us? You will be officially married to me. We will have a small, informal wedding ceremony where you'll marry all of us."

Caleb tried to keep his fear from showing. He was terrified she would turn them down. He knew she still didn't feel like she was going to get to stay with them, but they were just as determined she would. They wanted forever with her.

Lily looked down at the ring for several minutes, her mind in a confused haze. Could she do this? Could she marry them knowing it could end any day? She trembled at the thought of losing them. Then she remembered Helen's words about there being no guarantees in life. If they were willing to take a chance, could she do anything less than meet them halfway? Looking up into Caleb's eyes, she let her love shine through.

"Yes," she said softly before looking at Ethan and Allen, who sat holding their breath. "Yes, I'll marry you. All of you."

Ethan let out a loud whoop that startled all of them and had them laughing. Christmas had brought many wonderful presents. The most important one was them finding each other.

Chapter 16

Lily seemed to float through the next few days after Christmas. Helen had come over with some of her grandkids. She hugged Lily tightly when Lily had shown her the ring. After a furious snowball fight outside and hot chocolate to warm them up they had headed out. Helen promised she would be back after the first of the year and all her kids were gone. Lily had laughed at the exaggerated huff Helen had given. She knew Helen was going to miss having all the noise and activity.

Lily's smile quickly turned to a frown when she saw Ethan and Caleb talking furiously with one of the ranch hands. They seemed really upset. She waited until they came up the front steps before the curiosity became too much.

"What's wrong?" she asked anxiously.

"Several head of cattle have been found dead with bullet wounds to the head. We need to go check it out," Ethan said furious. "I need to call Matt to get his ass out here. Sorry, Lily," Ethan said as he pulled a quarter out of his pocket and dropped it into the cursing jar which was close to overflowing with quarters, dimes, nickels, and dollar bills. "Allen, can you call Matt and have him come out? We need to report this."

Allen had come in from the kitchen where he had gone to get a cup of coffee. "Sure. Where were they found?"

"In the pasture just a few miles from here. I'm surprised we didn't hear the shots with the way sound carries around here," Ethan said grimly. He was pissed at the senseless deaths. If he found out some of the local kids from town did this he was going to bust their asses, then make them work it off this summer.

Caleb came out with a couple of rifles and some additional ammo. He looked at Lily's concerned face and walked over to her. "It will be okay, baby. It's probably some kids who got a new gun for Christmas. This is just in case. Sometimes wolves come out if they smell fresh blood. We just need something to scare them off with."

Lily looked at the huge rifles and nodded silently. She put her hand on his cheek. "You'll be careful?"

Smiling down at her he gave her a quick kiss. "Always."

Lily looked at him, then at Ethan. "I love you both. Be careful for me."

Allen came up behind Lily and pulled her against him. "They will be, love. This is just a formality."

Lily nodded and watched as Ethan, Caleb and all the ranch hands in the yard except for Ed loaded up into their trucks and took off down the road. Allen kissed Lily gently on the top of her head. "Come back inside before you freeze."

Lily shivered. She had a bad feeling. She was scared. For some reason, she didn't think it was kids who had killed the livestock. Unwilling to share her fears with Allen in case he thought she was being silly, she smiled up at him before turning to go through to the kitchen.

"I think I'll put a roast in to cook for dinner tonight," Lily said as she moved through the dining room toward the kitchen.

"That sounds great. I have some paperwork I need to get done in the office. If you need me just call," Allen said.

"Allen," Lily said as she looked at him.

"Yes, baby."

"I love you," Lily said softly.

"I love you more," Allen said, staring at Lily for a moment before turning and walking down the hallway to the office.

Allen couldn't help the grin spreading across his face. He felt whole again. They were going to make plans for their wedding tonight. He and his brothers decided they didn't want to wait any longer than they had to. Lily might already be pregnant with their child. Even if she wasn't, they wanted to make sure she didn't have any excuses.

Heading toward the office, he remembered he needed to put a call into Matt. He didn't know where his mind was anymore. He snorted at the lie. He knew perfectly well where his mind was—on Lily.

He was just about to walk into the office when he felt the draft of cold air slice through the cracked door of the den. Frowning, he wondered if the weather stripping needed to be replaced. If so, he could get Ed to pick some up at the hardware store tomorrow.

Pushing open the door, he frowned at the opened French door. He had taken no more than two steps into the room when everything went dark. His last thought was he needed to protect Lily.

* * *

"I don't get it?" One of the ranch hands said as he moved around one of the dead cows. "You see this? This isn't your typical rifle. It was a high-powered rifle used more for military purposes. No kid is going to get that for Christmas."

Ethan frowned at the man talking. "How do you know?"

"I was in the army for twenty years, a sniper. If you look at the markings on the bullet you can tell a silencer was used. Whoever did this didn't want you to find it right away." The man held a bloody bullet in his hand after digging it out of the head of one of the cows.

"Shit. I don't like this, Ethan. Call Matt. Tell him to get to the house," Caleb said, already breaking into a run toward one of the trucks.

Ethan looked at the men with him. "You two take care of this. The rest of you get your asses back to the house. Use extreme caution."

The men nodded and scrambled for their trucks. Ethan pulled out his cell phone and called Matt, waiting impatiently until he picked up.

"Matt, did Allen call you?" Ethan asked breathlessly as he jumped into the passenger side seat as Caleb was pulling away.

"No. Why, is something wrong?" Matt asked.

"We had several of our cows shot. One of the ranch hands thinks it was with a sniper rifle. Allen was supposed to have called you over thirty minutes ago. We're heading back to the house now. Get there as soon as you can." Ethan could already hear the siren from Matt's truck in the background.

"On my way," Matt said, hanging up.

"Shit. Call the house," Caleb said trembling. He had to get to Lily. He had to know she was safe.

Ethan nodded, already dialing the phone. He let it ring until it went to the answering machine. "No answer. I'll call the office in the barn and see if Ed is there."

Ethan was just about to give up when he heard a weak voice say hello on the other end. "Ed. Ed, what the fuck is going on?"

"I don't know, boss man. I was sitting in the office minding my own business when I heard the horses kicking up a fit. When I went out to check on them, someone hit me over the head. Shit, that hurt. I can't get the door to open. They tied it closed from the outside."

"Stay put. We're on our way. So is Matt." Ethan hung up. He took a deep breath, trying to get his shaking under control. "Ed was attacked. He's locked in the office in the barn and can't get out," Ethan told his brother quietly.

Caleb just nodded, pressing down on the accelerator as far as he could without losing control. He couldn't help Lily if he killed them before they got there.

* * *

Peter Canton was pissed. It had taken them a lot longer than he expected to find the dead cattle. He had shot them two days ago. He had been waiting for news to hit the house and had been hiding in the loft of the barn, freezing his ass off. He had a hard time feeling his fucking fingers and toes. When he had finally heard the excitement and watched as the men had piled into their trucks and took off, he was ecstatic.

Now, there would just be the old man downstairs and the two in the house. He had already cased the house while they had been at the hospital after the bitch had thrown herself out of his car. He knew how he was going to break in and had even unlocked the door so he wouldn't have any problems.

Once he had taken care of the old man, he made his way to the back of the house. He would go in through the den. It had a set of French doors leading out onto the back part of the porch. He figured it would be the least used room in the house.

Opening the door, he moved into the room silently. He could hear the girl and the man talking in the living room. He thought he had hit pay dirt when he discovered they would be splitting up. The kitchen was on the other side of the house.

Peter grinned when he heard them express their love for each other. This would work to his advantage. When emotions were involved people would do anything to save a loved one. He would take out the man. Once he had him incapacitated, he could threaten him, and the girl would tell him everything.

Walking over to the door, he had just entered, he opened it just enough so the cold air would blow in. The office was across the hall. When the man came in to investigate why it was so cold he could take him out. Peter hid behind the door and waited.

Peter swung the wooden club he held, striking the man in the back of the head with a swift, hard blow as he walked through the door. He watched as the man named Allen crumbled to the floor. Reaching down, he grabbed Allen's arms and dragged him down the hall.

Using a large plastic zip tie, he threaded Allen's arms through the railing of the staircase and tied it tight. There was no way he was going to get loose. Now, he just needed to wait until Lily decided to join them.

He sat down in the chair in the corner facing the staircase. When Lily entered, she would see her lover, but not himself right away. Peter grinned. Soon he would live forever. He might even have a house or two like this one, only bigger.

* * *

Lily started dinner, but her thoughts kept straying to Allen. She wanted, no needed, to be near him. She fought her feelings for almost thirty minutes before she gave up.

Wiping her hands down the front of her apron, she took it off and hung it over the back of the chair. She missed the feel of Allen's arms around her. Maybe she could just go in on the pretense of taking him some more coffee.

Grinning at her quick thinking, she poured a cup of coffee and headed out through the dining room. She was standing in the doorway when she saw him lying against the stairs. Lily set the cup down on the table with a cry and rushed to where Allen lay so still. It wasn't until she was almost to him that she saw his hands were tied to the railing. She stopped suddenly and looked around fearfully.

"Now, don't stop. Your lover boy there needs to feel your sweet arms about him," a snide voice said from the corner of the living room.

Lily turned as Peter Canton stood up and took a couple of steps toward her. He motioned with his gun for her to go to Allen. Lily looked down at Allen, who had begun to moan, and hurried to his side.

Looking up, Lily looked into Peter's eyes. "What do you want?"

Peter frowned angrily at Lily. "I already told you what I wanted. Did you really think I would let you get away so easily? What did I tell you would happen if you didn't cooperate with me?"

Lily shivered. "Please, don't hurt him. I'll tell you everything I know. I'll go with you quietly. Just please, please, don't hurt him." She looked pleadingly into Peter's eyes. She would do anything to save Allen.

Peter grinned nastily. "You should have done that the first time. Now I have to teach you I mean what I say."

He raised his gun toward Allen, aiming for his leg. Lily's eyes grew large as she saw what he was about to do. Lily screamed as the gun went off.

Allen jerked at the sound of the gun exploding in the room, coming awake immediately. He roared when he couldn't move his arms. Struggling against the railing, he realized he felt something warm and wet on his leg. Looking down, his eyes widened in horror as he saw Lily lying across his legs.

"Lily? Lily, talk to me, baby," Allen pleaded, unable to move because of his arms being tied. "Lily, baby. Talk to me."

"Damn bitch," Peter Canton said furiously.

He hadn't expected the bitch to throw herself in front of the bastard he had tied. He had planned on shooting the son of a bitch in the leg to show he meant business. Lily had recognized his intent and thrown herself in front of the damn bastard, taking the bullet instead. Peter walked over and yanked on Lily's leg, pulling her away from the furious bastard he had tied up.

"Let her go, you bastard. I'm going to kill your fucking ass." Allen struggled against the strapping holding him, feeling the plastic cut deep into his wrists as he strained to get to Lily.

"Lily, talk to me, baby," Allen pleaded.

A trail of blood flowed across the floor where the man had dragged her. Peter gripped Lily's shoulder and turned her over. A dark stain covered her upper chest. Lily moaned as she was turned over.

Turning her head, she looked into Allen's eyes. "Allen," she said weakly.

"It's going to be all right, baby," Allen said. He turned his glare on the man standing over Lily. "What the fuck do you want?"

Peter looked at the man on the floor. "Immortality. I want to live forever like she does. She's going to tell me how she became immortal, or she's going to watch you die slowly right before her eyes."

"No. You mustn't hurt him," Lily said weakly, trying to pull herself up.

She struggled until she was sitting upright. She had to brace herself on one arm as a wave of dizziness swelled over her. She tried to draw in a deep breath to still the swirling room, but she was having trouble breathing.

* * *

Caleb, Ethan, and Matt had parked further down the road and come in on foot. They were almost to the barn when they heard the sound of a gunshot. Using the barn as cover, they surveyed the house.

Moving silently into the barn, Matt nodded to Caleb to go release Ed from the office while Ethan headed for the loft to make sure it was clear. Once it was determined it was, Matt came up to the loft to scope the house out. Pulling his rifle with its high-powered scope up onto his shoulder, he scanned the front rooms. A slight movement through the front windows got his attention, and he motioned for Ethan to take a look through his scope.

Ethan's breath caught in his throat when he saw his brother lying next to the staircase. Scanning the living room area, he saw Lily sitting on the floor and let out an expletive when he saw a dark stain that looked suspiciously like blood on the front of her sweater. He couldn't tell if the blood was hers or Allen's.

Just as he was about to scan for anyone else in the room Lily looked up, almost as if she knew he was there. Ethan's heart caught in his throat when she turned her head to the right as if she was looking at someone else in the room.

"Look to the right of Lily. I think she knows we are here. Can you get a clear shot?" Ethan said quietly to Matt.

"No, the lamp is in the way. I can't tell where he is," Matt cursed under his breath. If the son of a bitch would move just an inch in either direction he might have a clear shot.

Lily looked down at her trembling hand. It was covered in blood. She knew it was bad. She also knew Ethan and Caleb were out there waiting to save them.

Lily knew her time was up. There was no saving her, but there was a chance to save Allen.

Turning to look at Allen one last time, Lily's eyes filled with tears. Unable to speak for a moment, she let her love for him shine through her eyes before turning back to Peter.

"Help me up, and I'll tell you how to become immortal," Lily whispered faintly.

Allen stared at Lily in disbelief. He knew she had just told him good-bye, but he couldn't accept it. He wouldn't let her go.

"Lily. Goddammit. No. Do you hear me? Fucking no!" Allen shouted, struggling even more as silent tears flowed down his face. Dammit, he knew she was going to do something stupid. She had to listen to him.

Lily held out her hand for Peter to help her up. Waiting until he was halfway bent so he would be off balance, she threw her weight against him, forcing him out into the open and in front of the window. Peter had held onto the gun, and when Lily pushed him, he realized she was setting him up.

He raised his gun and fired just as a bullet shattered the front window. He was dead before he ever hit the floor. Lily stood still for a moment, shock holding her in place before she turned on unsteady feet and stumbled toward Allen. She sank down next to him slowly, laying her head down onto his legs.

Tears streamed down Allen's face as he kept saying over and over, "Oh no, baby, don't leave me. Don't leave me, baby."

Lily smiled faintly as she tried to focus on Allen's face. "I'll always be here. I'll find my way back. I will. Don't give up on me." Coughing, Allen's eyes closed as he saw the small stream of blood coming from the corner of Lily's mouth. He watched helplessly as Lily struggled for another breath. "Love you. Love you all so much. I'll come…" Lily's voice faded as her eyes went blank.

Allen stared down at Lily's wide-open eyes. He began shaking uncontrollably. An anguished cry ripped from his throat as he cried out his pain.

* * *

Ethan, Caleb, and Matt had run for the house as soon as they made the shot. They saw the bastard fall.

They had made it almost to the porch when Allen's anguished cry filled the air.

Bursting into the house, they rushed into the living room only to stand frozen as Allen fought against the restraints holding him, Lily's bloody and lifeless body lying across his lap.

Matt called in for the ambulance to come down the road as he went over and sliced through the ties holding Allen. Ethan and Caleb walked slowly toward them in disbelief. Allen gathered Lily in his arms as soon as he was free, gently smoothing her hair away from her face. Ethan and Caleb sank to their knees next to Allen and Lily, touching her, begging her to come back to them, telling her over and over they were not ready for her to go. They told her how much they needed her. They even cursed a blue streak trying to get her to respond, but nothing they did could wake her up this time.

She had known she wouldn't be allowed to stay, but they had hoped they could prove her wrong. They loved her so much they had felt certain nothing could take her away, but they had been wrong. Their Lily was gone.

Chapter 17

Matt twisted his hat in his hands as he looked at the three men sitting and standing in the room with him. Sometimes he really, really hated his job, and right now was one of those times.

He had driven out to the ranch to let them know that Lily's body had been misplaced. The ambulance had delivered her body to the hospital, and she had been transferred to the morgue. But when Doc Harley went down to confirm the death and make a ruling as to how she had died, her body was nowhere to be found. An intensive search was still underway, but Matt had a feeling they wouldn't find anything.

Ethan sat at his desk in the office staring into space. Caleb sat with his arms on his knees, staring at the floor, and Allen stood with his back to Matt, staring out the window. It had been two days since Lily had died in his arms, and he still hadn't spoken to anyone, not even his brothers. He just stared out the window like he was waiting for Lily to come home.

January

February

March

April

May 23rd

Life on the ranch had returned to normal as much as it could. There was still some light snow on the ground, but the days were getting longer and it was beginning to warm up a little more. Helen had been acting as their housekeeper since Lily's death.

The brothers had learned to rely on each other to get through the pain of losing Lily. At first, Allen had been sure she would return any day, but as days turned to weeks and weeks to months he began to lose hope. They had read her journal over and over, hoping to find some clue in the first few days after her death until one day they went to get it and it was gone, along with her big canvas bag.

That was when all three of them had broken down and cried. They ranted and raved at God for not even letting them have some small part of her. They had no place to visit to say their good-byes, nothing to remind them she had even been there. Maggie had flown in from Florida for a visit during their last bad time. Helen hadn't known what to do so she had called for reinforcements. The pain she saw in them was more than she could handle.

"What the hell are you boys doing? You had better not run Helen off, you hear me?" Maggie snapped at the three of them as they sat at the table.

"Why, dammit, Maggie? Why? Why couldn't we even have some small piece to remember her by?" Allen asked, his voice choked.

"But, she did leave a piece of her behind. It's all around you, Allen. You just can't see it. Look at the three of you. Before she came, you were all so absorbed in your own problems you didn't recognize the pain each of you were feeling. Now, all three of you are working through it together. You've become a family. You can see the difference in the house. It isn't just a house anymore, it's a home. You just need to look around you. All three of you. She left a lot of herself here."

"We miss her so much, Maggie. We miss her so much each and every day," Ethan said quietly.

"I know, Ethan," Maggie replied softly. She gathered her jacket. "You boys get on with your chores. I need to run into town. I haven't seen Gladys since I came in, and if I'm going to be here I better go get some grub for everyone."

"Maggie," Caleb said quietly. "Thanks for coming. We missed you."

Maggie smiled sadly at the boys, her heart going out to them. They were in a lot of pain, but they were working through it together. She walked down the steps and had a vague sense of déjà vu. Looking up at the sky, she couldn't resist having a little conversation with God. Not too unlike what she'd had before.

"You know I'm not much for making demands or talking to you, but I've got a little complaint. If'n you were the one who sent Lily, she was supposed to stay until the boys no longer needed her. From the looks of it, they need her more now than ever. Lily said she wouldn't leave until the boys didn't need her anymore. Well, they still need her bad, so I think you need to think about sending her back as she hasn't finished the job you sent her on. Now, if you want to take offense to an old woman's scolding, you go right on ahead, but if you look at those boys you'll see I'm right." Maggie paused a minute before she said a little more softly. "Please send Lily back. I think she needs my boys as much as they need her."

Shaking her head at her own lunacy, she climbed into the truck and headed to town. She had to admit she didn't think it would work, but what the hell, it couldn't hurt anything to ask. She drove to town, pulling into the parking space in front of the diner. She slowly climbed from the truck and walked in, not really knowing what to do if her wish didn't come true.

"Afternoon, Gladys. Hey, Earl. Hey, Carl," Maggie called out, heading for the back booth. Gladys smiled as Maggie came in and poured a couple cups of coffee.

"Hey, Maggie. How are the boys doing?" Gladys asked as she eased into the seat across from her.

"Not too good," Maggie said sadly. "They really loved that girl."

"I knew they would," Gladys said as she sipped her coffee. "You know, I heard tell the strangest story about her from Becky at the sheriff's station."

Gladys went on to tell Maggie about how Matt had a report on Lily only this Lily had been born in 1901. Maggie listened intently to the story, her eyes widening in wonder. If it was true, then just maybe there was a way to bring Lily back to the boys. Maggie's eyes gleamed. Maybe her talk to God wouldn't be in vain. If one wish brought her to them in the first place, maybe another one would do the same. It never hurt to try.

She and Gladys spent the next hour catching up on what had happened while Maggie was in Florida. Maggie was just finishing her coffee when the bell over the door chimed. A small figure came into the diner and walked up to the booth where she and Gladys were sitting.

"Excuse me. You wouldn't happen to know of anyone looking for a housekeeper, would you?" a soft voice asked.

Lily watched as Maggie's eyes grew wide, then filled with tears. In a shaky voice, Maggie replied, "I might. There are these three men, but they need a lot of love and someone who won't take off when they start growling."

Lily smiled softly. "Seems like they need more than a housekeeper."

Maggie nodded. "Yes. Do you think you'll be up to the job? They need someone who is going to be willing to stay a long, long time."

Lily's smile grew. "Oh, yes. I'm up for the job. From the sound of it, it might take a lifetime to get them back in shape."

"Oh, Lily. He heard my prayer," Maggie whispered.

"He wasn't the only one who heard," Lily replied softly. "Maggie, will you please take me home?"

Chapter 18

Lily wrung her hands nervously on the ride back to the ranch. She didn't know what to expect. Would they still want her? Lily stared out of the window anxiously, impatient to get to the ranch.

"Do you think they will still want me?" Lily asked, biting her lip. "I miss them so much."

"Honey, those boys love you," Maggie assured her. "There's not a day that goes by they don't wish you were with them. I swear, I'll be surprised if they ever let you out of their sight again once they see you."

Lily shone a beautiful smile at Maggie. "Oh, Maggie. I don't ever want to be away from them again."

"Here we are," Maggie said with a contented sigh. "The boys don't look like they are back yet. They went over to the old homestead to finish the repairs on the barn. They should be home any time, though. Let's get you settled in."

Lily tried to hide her disappointment. Maybe this was for the best. It would give her time to get in control of her emotions before facing them. Just going back into the house held such potent memories.

Lily walked slowly up the steps, pausing before going through the double front doors. She clutched her canvas bag tight against her chest. As she walked across the threshold she felt like she was finally coming home.

"Go take your stuff up to the master bedroom and then come meet me in the kitchen. We can get some dinner going while we wait, and you can talk to me," Maggie said, carrying a bag of groceries into the kitchen.

"I'll be right down," Lily said breathlessly.

She ran her hand along the staircase, loving the feel of the rich wood under it. As she climbed the stairs, her smile grew as she remembered Caleb carrying her up the stairs on Christmas morning. She looked down at the sapphire and diamond ring on her left hand. It was the morning they had asked her to marry them.

She shivered as she remembered how they had made love to her on the rug in front of the fire. Afterward, Caleb had bathed with her in the large sunken tub. They had ended up making love again, slower, almost tentatively. It had been so beautiful wrapped in his strong arms.

Lily walked into the master bedroom and looked around. None of the men had left their things in the room. She went to the walk-in closet and opened it. The things she had bought were hanging neatly on hangers or folded on the shelf, almost like she had never left. She wanted to fill the closet with their things next to hers.

Lily closed her eyes as a sharp pain swept through her. She loved them so much. Impatiently, she put her things in the closet. Taking her journal, she laid it on the nightstand next to the huge bed. Lily's lips curved with a slight smile as she ran her hand over the covers. She had plans for the bed tonight, and it didn't include sleeping.

Leaving the room, Lily practically floated down the stairs to the kitchen. Curled on a pillow under the window was Edison. Her kitten had grown up.

"Oh, Edison. Look at you. You've grown up so much," Lily said as she leaned over to pet him. Edison stretched lazily, looked at her with a disgruntled meow, and closed his eyes again.

Lily laughed. "Well, he seems content."

"The boys don't admit to spoiling him. Ed is just as bad. I guess every time someone would take him out to the barn to live he would disappear, and they would find him back in here trying to get into your old room," Maggie said as she put a meatloaf into the oven.

Lily wrapped an apron around her slim waist and picked up a potato to wash and cut up for mashed potatoes.

"Lily, where did you go?" Maggie asked hesitantly. She wasn't sure if it was something she should ask or not, but damn, she was curious as hell.

Lily paused a moment and stared out the window before answering. "I don't really know. It is like a dream world. The colors are all so vibrant." Lily looked down as she picked up another potato. "It looks a lot like it looks here, only more."

Maggie thought about what Lily said before asking another question. "You said God wasn't the only one who heard my prayer. Who else heard?"

Lily looked at Maggie with a soft smile. "Let's just say there were quite a few people in heaven who heard you. Your brothers told me to tell you hello."

Maggie's eyes filled with tears at the mention of Ethan, Allen, and Caleb's dads. Her chin trembled a little before she sniffed and turned back to get some rolls out of the freezer. Lily, while in the dream world that was her life between her missions on earth, had finally met Adam, Jake, and Emily Cunnings. They had watched over their boys, worrying about them. When Maggie had sent her initial prayer it had been them, and to her surprise, her Momma and Da, who had encouraged Lily to be the one sent to them. When Lily had returned she had been inconsolable. If not for the support of her Momma and Da, she felt certain she would have sunk to the realms of purgatory. She had been a lost soul.

Time was irrelevant in her dream world. She had been shocked to discover almost five months had passed since she had left. Wiping her hands down her apron, she trembled at the thought of them being apart for so many months. What if they had decided to move on? What if they had decided she wasn't worth the wait?

Maggie's head came up as she listened. "I hear the truck. They're back. Go to them, Lily. Go to them, honey," Maggie said, encouraging Lily. She helped Lily take off her apron and smiled as Lily nervously brushed her hands over her hair. "You look beautiful. Go on."

Lily nodded. She walked slowly through the dining room and stood by the front window watching as the truck pulled in and backed up to the barn. Her breath caught in her throat as she watched them getting out of the cab of the truck. Her hand slowly moved to her throat, and she held back a sob.

She moved to the front door and opened it. She slowly walked down the steps, never taking her eyes off where the men had gone. They were unloading the back of the pickup.

Lily was halfway across the yard when Allen appeared out of the barn, heading to pick up another stack of lumber. He looked so tall and handsome. His light brown hair was peeking out from under his cowboy hat, and he had a slight shadow of a beard like he hadn't shaved this morning. His jacket was open, showing the dark blue shirt stretched across his broad shoulders. He was wearing his trademark blue jeans and boots.

* * *

Allen was tired. He couldn't sleep more than a couple of hours each night before the nightmares came. He didn't know how much longer he could go on. He didn't know how much longer he wanted to go on without Lily. It seemed like every time he closed his eyes all he could see was her lying across his legs, bloody and lifeless, while he could do nothing but call out to her.

He had lost weight again and was to the point he just wanted to give up. Maybe in death he could be with her. He fought with his feelings, knowing how devastating it would be to his brothers, so he kept trying to put one foot in front of the other. It was just getting so damn hard to do.

Coming out of the barn, he was focusing on trying to get the materials they hadn't used out of the truck. He didn't even want to think about the fact it was getting dark. Dark meant sleep and sleep meant nightmares.

As he headed for the back of the truck to pick up more materials, he felt like he was being watched. Thinking it was Maggie back, he glanced up and the world seemed to fade away. Standing before him was Lily, more beautiful than ever.

The pain that lanced through him took his breath away. He closed his eyes and took in a deep breath, trying to get the pain under control. Opening his eyes slowly, he watched as the vision of Lily walked slowly toward him. It was only when he heard his name that he was able to move, first one step, then another until he was almost running. Vaguely he heard a sound that sounded like a sob, but he couldn't tell where it was coming from until he felt the chill on his cheeks from the tears running down his face.

Lily was unsure of what to do when Allen first saw her. He glanced up as if realizing he was under scrutiny, his eyes going wide with disbelief before he closed them. When he closed his eyes, she was afraid he would open them to look at her with a cold indifference. Instead, she had seen the same pain she had felt at being torn apart from them.

"Oh, Allen," Lily whispered just loud enough for him to hear.

She ran toward him, throwing herself into his arms and wrapping her arms tightly around his neck while her legs wrapped around his waist. She buried her face in his neck and took a deep breath to absorb his unique scent. She loved how he smelled. She loved being in his arms. She never wanted to be apart from him again.

Lifting her tear-laden eyes to him, she pulled his head down to kiss her. She definitely loved the taste of him. Kissing him over and over, she was gasping for breath when he finally pulled her back far enough so he could look down into her face.

Touching her almost with relevance, he whispered. "Lily?"

"Oh, Allen. I've missed you so much," Lily whispered back huskily. "I love you so much." She kissed him again deeply.

* * *

Ethan was worried about both his brothers. He knew Allen wasn't sleeping at night. Hell, none of them were. They each tried to fool the other, but even in a house the size of theirs, it was impossible to hide the small noises they made during the night.

All of them had lost weight, but both Allen and Caleb seemed to have lost even more; they had lost their desire to live. Running his hand down his face, he had to admit he was not far behind them. The house just seemed to be so empty without Lily's presence. He hated going to an empty bed each night after remembering holding her soft, sweet body against his. Nothing seemed to give him pleasure any more. He moved more as a robot than a man. He only wondered when this hell would finally end.

Looking around, he frowned when he realized Allen hadn't come back in with another load. They had been acting as an assembly line with Allen getting the wood out of the truck and handing it to him and him handing it up to Caleb in the loft. Telling Caleb he would be right back, he took off out of the barn at a run.

The three of them had hardly let each other out of their sight for fear of what one of them might do in a moment of weakness. Ethan skidded to a stop when he saw his brother holding someone in his arms, or rather, holding someone who was wrapped around him like garland on a Christmas tree. His heart thumping in his chest, he slowed to a walk as he stared at the hint of long dark brown hair hanging down over his brother's shoulder. It wasn't until the vision looked up that he saw her face. Numbly, he walked like a zombie toward them.

Lily smiled down at Allen when he pulled her back far enough to look at her. Out of the corner of her eye she saw movement. Turning her head, she watched as Ethan came out of the barn almost running. When he saw them he slowed. Lily looked at

Ethan and smiled, her love for him shining out of her eyes.

"Ethan!" she breathed, sliding her legs down Allen's.

Allen turned her slightly, reluctant to let go of her. He held her close until Ethan was close enough to touch her, and only then did he release her, making sure his brother had her first.

Lily flowed into Ethan's arms, looking up at his darkly handsome face. His hair was a touch longer than he used to wear it. Lily pulled his hat off so she could run her fingers through the thick fullness of his black hair. She stared up into his rich brown eyes, drowning in the love she saw there. Throwing her arms up around his broad shoulders, she held on as he lifted her up against his chest and kissed her like a man starving.

"Oh, Ethan. I love you so much," Lily said between kisses. "I love you. I love you. I love you," she kept repeating as she returned his kisses.

Ethan's broad shoulders shook as he sobbed. He had his Lily again. He was never going to let her go again. She belonged to them.

"You're staying, Lily. Never again will you leave us. Never again. I can't live without you." Ethan's arms wrapped around her so tightly she had trouble breathing, but she wasn't complaining. He could hold her as tight as he wanted. She never wanted to be out of his strong arms ever again.

"What the hell are you guys doing? It's getting dark, and we still have a shitload of wood to put up," Caleb called out as he came out of the barn.

Ethan lowered Lily down to the ground, still retaining her hand in his as he turned to look at his younger brother.

"Caleb, you owe me fifty cents," Lily said in a trembling voice.

Caleb froze when he heard Lily's voice, unable to move. He began trembling as he stared at her. He moaned, slowly sinking to his knees, his hands on his thighs as he cried out in anguish.

Caleb felt like he had finally cracked. He was not only hearing her voice but seeing her. The pain was more than he could handle. He didn't want to fight it any longer. He wanted to let it sweep him away. He couldn't take any more. Life without Lily wasn't worth living.

Weeping, he hunched his shoulders in defeat. Filled with shame that he would disappoint his brothers, he just couldn't do it any longer. A soft, delicate hand caressed his face gently wiping the tears flowing in silent streaks down his cheeks.

"Caleb, I love you so much. Look at me, baby. Look at me. Hold me. Don't ever let me go," Lily kept saying as she placed both of her palms against his cold cheeks, forcing him to look up into her eyes. "I need you, baby. Forever."

Caleb stared at Lily as if he couldn't believe his own eyes. It was only when she pressed her lips against his that he realized she was really there. She was holding him, touching him. She was really there.

His hands touched her as if afraid she would disappear if he tried to hold her too tight. When she moaned and moved even closer, he gathered her closer to his body, kissing her as if he would never stop. Lily lay halfway across Caleb's lap, her hair draped over his arm, pressed tightly against his chest, while he kissed her face and hair and ran his hands over her cheeks and down her shoulder.

"Uh, Caleb," Lily whispered, turning pink. "I think we have an audience."

Caleb could have cared less. He touched Lily's pink cheeks in wonder. She was really here. In his arms.

Allen and Ethan laughed out loud, looking around as more and more smiling faces appeared as news of Lily's return spread. Maggie stood on the steps of the porch with tears running down her face. Ed had called Clive and Helen, and they were just pulling up. Helen jumped out of the truck with a cry. Brad and Harold leaned against the truck with huge grins on their faces, wondering if they could put in a prayer or two for an angel to call their own.

Caleb helped Lily up and swung her into his arms, twirling her around and around while whooping it up. Ethan and Allen took turns holding her before handing her back into Caleb's waiting arms. Dinner was a hurried affair with Maggie finally shooing the four of them off to bed.

Pulling her coat on, she made the decision to go into town to spend some quality time with Gladys. She had a feeling she wouldn't be getting much sleep if she decided to stay the night there. Yup, Florida had really nice weather in May. Before leaving, she looked up and said a silent "thank you."

Epilogue

Lily closed the journal, laying it aside as she stared out the window at the snow-capped mountains. She had been back almost a year. It was so hard to believe. Time seemed to speed by.

She looked at the new pictures on the tables in the den. Her wedding pictures and other pictures filled the room. They had had a lovely wedding. She had said her official wedding vows marrying her to Caleb, then Ethan and Allen had come to stand next to her, surrounding her as they each said the vows they had written for each other. Lily had framed them and hung them alongside the pictures. She felt so loved that sometimes she felt like her heart would swell and burst.

She smiled and leaned back when she felt arms slide around her waist to pull her back against a hard body. Looking up into Ethan's dark eyes, she saw the same love for her shining from him. He slid his hand down and over her rounded stomach, feeling the baby kicking under the palm of his hand.

He had been right. She was even more beautiful rounded with their child. One of the men was always with her in the same room. At first, they were afraid she would rebel, feeling they were suffocating her, but she never complained. She seemed to need to be with them as much as they needed to be with her.

Even at night they all slept in the same room, the men never quite able to let go of the fear of losing her. Lily didn't mind in the least. She wrapped her hands over Ethan's threading her fingers through his.

"Lily." Allen and Caleb stood in the doorway, a grin on their face. "Guess what we got in the mail today? An early Christmas present. Want to see what it is?"

Lily squealed as Ethan swung her up into his arms with a wicked grin. "She sure does. She has been a very, very naughty girl."

To be continued:
Touching Rune: Second Chance Book 2

Preview of *Touching Rune*

(Second Chance: Book 2)

Synopsis

Rune August embraces her life in New York City in 1894. She has lived again and again through many different time periods, but has never found tranquility until she walked into St. Agnes Home for Orphans. In her heart, she believes she has found a place she can call home. She will do everything she can to give the children in the orphanage a better life.

When a developer sets his sights on the property she and the children call home, she doesn't hesitate to fight back - and win. But that win comes at a terrible price... her life... casting her once again into the shadows.

Refusing to leave the children unprotected, she watches over and protects them in a different form... as the beloved statue in their center garden. But her time as the children's guardian angel draws to a close when the orphanage is renovated. Rune finds herself packed away and sold. Her new home is now far away from the familiar streets of New York and the children she loves.

Sergei Vasiliev and his best friend and bodyguard, Dimitri Mihailov, run one of the most powerful computer software development companies in the world. Both men carry deep scars from their life on the streets and from living in the world of the ultra-rich. Sergei knows men want him for his power and women want him for his money. Dimitri knows that some men and women would do anything to gain the secrets their company is developing.

Their lives change when Sergei purchases a statue for their home outside of Moscow. There is something about the statue of the young woman that touches an unexpected need deep inside both of them.

An impulsive purchase and a simple wish will change their lives forever. For anyone who touches Rune learns that love and hope are what makes the world a better place. Can she warm the hearts of two bitter, scarred men before the last petal falls from the Christmas rose that grows in the garden that has become her new home or will she be forever frozen, destined to only love them from afar?

If you loved this story by me (S.E. Smith) please leave a review. You can also take a look at additional books and sign up for my newsletter at **http://sesmithfl.com** to hear about my latest releases or keep in touch using the following links:

Website: http://sesmithfl.com
Newsletter: http://sesmithfl.com/?s=newsletter
Facebook: https://www.facebook.com/se.smith.5
Twitter: https://twitter.com/sesmithfl
Pinterest: http://www.pinterest.com/sesmithfl/
Blog: http://sesmithfl.com/blog/
Forum: http://www.sesmithromance.com/forum/

Excerpts of S.E. Smith Books

If you would like to read more S.E. Smith stories, she recommends Touch of Frost, the first in her Magic, New Mexico series. Or if you prefer Westerns with a twist or Sci-fi, you can check out Indiana Wild or Abducting Abby…

Additional Books by S.E. Smith

Short Stories and Novellas
For the Love of Tia
(Dragon Lords of Valdier Book 4.1)
A Dragonling's Easter
(Dragonlings of Valdier Book 1.1)
A Dragonling's Haunted Halloween
(Dragonlings of Valdier Book 1.2)

A Dragonling's Magical Christmas
(Dragonlings of Valdier Book 1.3)
A Warrior's Heart
(Marastin Dow Warriors Book 1.1)
Rescuing Mattie
(Lords of Kassis: Book 3.1)

Science Fiction/Paranormal Novels

Cosmos' Gateway Series

Tink's Neverland (Cosmos' Gateway: Book 1)
Hannah's Warrior (Cosmos' Gateway: Book 2)
Tansy's Titan (Cosmos' Gateway: Book 3)
Cosmos' Promise (Cosmos' Gateway: Book 4)
Merrick's Maiden (Cosmos' Gateway Book 5)

Curizan Warrior

Ha'ven's Song (Curizan Warrior: Book 1)

Dragon Lords of Valdier

Abducting Abby (Dragon Lords of Valdier: Book 1)
Capturing Cara (Dragon Lords of Valdier: Book 2)
Tracking Trisha (Dragon Lords of Valdier: Book 3)
Ambushing Ariel (Dragon Lords of Valdier: Book 4)
Cornering Carmen (Dragon Lords of Valdier: Book 5)
Paul's Pursuit (Dragon Lords of Valdier: Book 6)
Twin Dragons (Dragon Lords of Valdier: Book 7)

Lords of Kassis Series

River's Run (Lords of Kassis: Book 1)
Star's Storm (Lords of Kassis: Book 2)
Jo's Journey (Lords of Kassis: Book 3)
Ristéard's Unwilling Empress (Lords of Kassis: Book 4)

Magic, New Mexico Series

Touch of Frost (Magic, New Mexico Book 1)
Taking on Tory (Magic, New Mexico Book 2)

Sarafin Warriors

Choosing Riley (Sarafin Warriors: Book 1)

Viper's Defiant Mate (Sarafin Warriors Book 2)

The Alliance Series

Hunter's Claim (The Alliance: Book 1)

Razor's Traitorous Heart (The Alliance: Book 2)

Dagger's Hope (The Alliance: Book 3)

Zion Warriors Series

Gracie's Touch (Zion Warriors: Book 1)

Krac's Firebrand (Zion Warriors: Book 2)

Paranormal and Time Travel Novels

Spirit Pass Series

Indiana Wild (Spirit Pass: Book 1)

Spirit Warrior (Spirit Pass Book 2)

Second Chance Series

Lily's Cowboys (Second Chance: Book 1)

Touching Rune (Second Chance: Book 2)

Young Adult Novels

Breaking Free Series

Voyage of the Defiance (Breaking Free: Book 1)

Recommended Reading Order Lists:

http://sesmithfl.com/reading-list-by-events/

http://sesmithfl.com/reading-list-by-series/

About S.E. Smith

S.E. Smith is a *New York Times, USA TODAY, International, and Award-Winning* Bestselling author of science fiction, fantasy, paranormal, and contemporary works for adults, young adults, and children. She enjoys writing a wide variety of genres that pull her readers into worlds that take them away.

CPSIA information can be obtained
at www.ICGtesting.com
Printed in the USA
BVHW091228210219
540827BV00020B/742/P